4/11
9/14
7/10

The Whispering Rod

A Tale of Old Massachusetts

A Novel
by
Nancy Kelley

WHITE MANE KIDS
SHIPPENSBURG, PENNSYLVANIA

This White Mane Books publication
was printed by
Beidel Printing House, Inc.
63 West Burd Street
Shippensburg, PA 17257-0708 USA

The acid-free paper used in this book meets the guidelines for permanence and durability of the Committee on Production Guidelines for Book Longevity of the Council on Library Resources.

For a complete list of available publications
please write
White Mane Books
Division of White Mane Publishing Company, Inc.
P.O. Box 708
Shippensburg, PA 17257-0708 USA

Library of Congress Cataloging-in-Publication Data

Kelley, Nancy, 1955-
    The whispering rod : a tale of old Massachusetts : a novel / by Nancy Kelley.
        p. cm.
    Summary: In 1659, fourteen-year-old Hannah Pryor is troubled by the persecution of Quakers by Puritan Boston's leading citizens, one of whom is her father, especially after learning of her deceased mother's friendship with a Quaker woman.
    ISBN 1-57249-248-1 (alk. paper)
    1. Boston (Mass.)--History--Colonial period, ca. 1600-1775--Juvenile fiction. [1. Boston (Mass.)--History--Colonial period, ca. 1600-1775--Fiction. 2. Puritans--Fiction. 3. Quakers--Fiction. 4. Christian life--History--17th century--Fiction. 5. Frontier and pioneer life--Massachusetts--Fiction. 6. Massachusetts--History--Colonial period, ca. 1600-1775--Fiction.] I. Title.

PZ7.K28173 Wh 2001
[Fic]--dc21

2001026797

For Chris, Ruth, Kathy and Susan whose friendship, insights and quiet prodding made this book possible.

Contents

Prologue vi

Chapter 1 The Town Spring 1

Chapter 2 The Prisoners 8

Chapter 3 Reprieved 16

Chapter 4 Scandal Close to Home 24

Chapter 5 The Letter... 32

Chapter 6 Goody Hawkins 40

Chapter 7 Anne Hutchinson................................. 47

Chapter 8 Sunday Meeting 58

Chapter 9 The Tavern 65

Chapter 10 Preacher in the Wilderness.................. 73

Chapter 11 Winter.. 84

Chapter 12 An Unlikely Friend 91

Chapter 13 Consequences 102

Chapter 14 The Verdict 108

Chapter 15 Day of Reckoning 117

Chapter 16 The Decision 122

Chapter 17 The Whispering Rod 129

Chapter 18 The *Griffin* 136

Chapter 19 Farewell 144

Chapter 20 A New Beginning 151

Chapter 21 Forgiveness 160

Afterword 163

Bibliography 165

Prologue

I write this story to no one in particular. My words are unimportant and my script is not one bit pretty, all pointed and crabbed—like the scratching of a hen, as Mistress Gibbons says. But I do not attend her dame's school any longer. I am too old for that now. In any case, Father is a better teacher. He thinks a girl should read and write as well as a boy as long as she does not neglect her duties. He does not mind then, that I write by the light of my betty lamp even though it is well past bedtime. Or that ink is dear, and he needs it to keep his books. That is the one task, when he lets me, that I truly enjoy—making entries in his leather-bound ledger—for Father is a joiner with many good customers. Some pay for his fine woodworking with coin and others with barter—hens, butter, bolts of cloth, and the like. Each exchange must be duly noted and rightly tallied, so that those worthy of credit are known from those who are not. I think the ink that I write with now is a reward for my efforts on Father's behalf—my tightly scripted handwriting being perfectly suited to the meticulous demands of a ledger's columns. If only Mistress Gibbons could see the practicality of my industry. I doubt that she would be swayed, however, to see me working with numbers, like a tradesman. If the truth be known, the thing I like best about keeping the ledger is what you learn about the people in the town. It tells you more than you would imagine, if you really look at it as I do.

Often there is no one to tell things to, so I tell them to myself, in this way, in this simple daybook. It is wonderful Providence that its pages were left unmarked, except for the days of the week in margins ruled by her own hand. My mother's hand. Perhaps she hears my thoughts or reads my words. It is folly, I know, to think such things and an abomination to imagine the dead among the living. But I have had a troubled mind of late, and to write in the calm of the evening by lamplight gives me comfort. In that, surely there can be no harm.

Chapter One

The Town Spring

It began that day at the town spring. I arrived with yoke and buckets to collect the day's water and to wash but a handful of linens in the creek. It was a fine morning for washing—brilliant autumn colors stretched across a clear October sky. After so wet and dreary a week, I could hardly mind the task at all for setting me out-of-doors again. I lay down my heavy load and looked about. Three goodwives huddled nearby at the edge of the creek. They spoke in excited voices, hushing one another from time to time as though to keep the matter from the children who ran and flitted about. That, and the extra vigor they put to scrubbing their linens, told me that this was not the usual gossip. I know it is wicked to eavesdrop, but I could not help but step a little closer. Three wide skirts wiggled to the motion of the chore, and I daresay I nearly had to cover a large grin, except that it disappeared quickly when I heard these words:

"Heretic."

"Jezebel."

"The Devil's harlot."

A twig snapped loudly beneath my shoe. One by one they turned—first, Patience Burrows who elbowed Nellie Colburn who tipped her head to Constance Brown. I bade them each a proper good morning.

1

"Good morning, Hannah Pryor," each replied in turn, nodding white-capped heads as they looked me over from head to toe. Mindful of myself, I took up the buckets but gingerly, for a mean blister had started and I did not want them attending me over it. Goody Burrows would prescribe a remedy—boiling the root of a parsnip with mud from the chicken yard, or some such thing. Goody Colburn would instruct me on the proper way to balance the yoke. Goody Brown, who could never find pity enough to go around, would offer to carry the load herself. I wanted not a fuss, but for the goodwives to continue so that I could learn the name of the woman who had fallen so low.

"Have ye heard the news, Hannah?" said Goody Colburn, rising slowly from her knees and putting her hand to the small of her back.

"Why, no," I said as easy like as I could.

"Mistress Samuels was safe delivered of a son last night. Thanks to the good Lord and the ministering of Patience Burrows."

"Why, this is good news, indeed," I said, turning to Goody Burrows with a smile, yet thinking, this cannot be! The saintly Mistress Samuels a heretic, a Jezebel?

"Fortunately, I didn't tarry long with her," said Goody Burrows, rising with agility and pushing dampened sleeves up great forearms. "A good draught of sugar and mint leaves dulls the pain."

"Mistress Samuels rests well, then?" I asked.

"Quite well, dear."

"And the child?"

"A healthy son. Mistress Samuels praised the Lord for number six, but I'm not so sure she wasn't lookin' for a daughter!"

Still, I was confounded and tried to think of how I might ask of this woman without being forward, when Goody Brown spoke.

"She knows not how fortunate she is to have sons. With five daughters, my husband and I hope that the Lord sees fit to pass around plenty of fine features so they won't be wantin' for husbands."

"It's not charm they need, but good strong backs!" said Patience Burrows. She laughed huskily, showing the enormous gap between her two front teeth. An ample bosom, ruddy complexion, and pumpkin-colored hair might give Goody Burrows a jovial appearance, but I thought her a busybody with a taste for the coarse and bossy, too.

"And ye know," she added with a wink. "She has the finest childbirth linen I ever did see! Embellished with embroidery! From England!"

"Imagine!" exclaimed Nellie Colburn, in her high-minded way.

"My, my," said Constance Brown with a palm to her cheek.

"And the child's christening gown...of the purest silk, and—"

"Fitting for a magistrate's son, as it should be," interrupted Goody Colburn. She had a habit of punctuating her opinion with a sniff of her long, sharp nose.

"Yes, as it should be," agreed Goody Brown meekly.

"Or a mollycoddle, like the rest of them boys is!" quipped Goody Burrows. The other goodwives laughed, because the truth of it is, they agree with Goody Burrows' more common way of thinking, especially when it comes to the business of the more prosperous folk in town.

By then it was apparent to me that I was not to be let in on the secret. To ask outright would have been a brazen thing to do, so I listened instead as they went on about Mistress Samuels' other fine possessions—her silver tea set, the cushions on the chamber chairs, and the curtains and vallens on her bed made of the finest worsted camlet—until I grew weary of such talk and gathered up my linens—

Father's good shirt, a petticoat and stockings, and some kitchen rags.

I went to the edge of the creek and dipped my hand to test the water. Powerful cold it was, and I pulled away, sitting back on my heels in the grass. All around red and yellow leaves danced a jig in the morning light. It made me a little sad to think it was their last merriment. Soon, they would turn to burgundy and gold and be gone. Nevertheless, the sun had yet the power to warm, so I closed my eyes and put my face to it.

The next thing I knew, Patience Burrows had plunked her large person down beside me and submerged a muslin sheet into the creek with her big, chapped hands.

"Woolgathering again, are ye, Hannah?"

I smiled politely at the remark, casting a sidelong look to see if it were Mistress Samuels' childbirth linen. The water ran dark with blood. I looked away. Goody Burrows gave me a knowing smirk.

"Hannah, I believe it's time you learned the ways of a midwife."

This made me feel like a silly girl and a child; I did not reply. Nellie Colburn, ever in contention with Patience Burrows, came to my defense.

"Hannah is a good daughter with little idle time what with keeping house for Goodman Pryor. No need to start someone so young on midwifery. There's time enough for that."

"Motherless girls need instruction in the physical necessities," replied Goody Burrows with her usual boldness. "And what better way is there, I ask you, than leading the calf straight to the udder?"

"Perhaps she should become a goodwife first, then a *midwife*," suggested Constance Brown.

Goody Brown rarely challenged Goody Burrows on any point, least of all on the subject of her specialty. I could not help but show the flicker of a smile for her boldness even through my discomfit.

"Would do her no harm," huffed Goody Burrows. "How else will she learn living with her father alone and all?"

They continued to talk about me as though I were not standing there in plain sight. It was just as well since I wanted no part of Goody Burrows' offer. Surely her intentions were good. So were those of the other goodwives. Ever since my own mother died on the very day I was born, they had tried to make up for the loss, instructing and scolding as they saw fit. They had taught me how to manage a household, to cook and to sew, to carry myself properly on Sundays. Still, some things come hard, like keeping the fire stoked so the bread won't fall or pulling at the innards of a chicken after Father has killed it, as though the guts are anything but warm and slick and all but alive. I say not a word about it, for I must do better. I must not be so terrible timid. Not even about the things that frighten me most, like sickness. And childbirth. When I stand beside the goodwives with their strong shoulders and capable hands, I feel so small and weak. I cannot imagine that they ever find the day's toil arduous or that they are scarcely able to read the Bible at eventide for the sleep that overcomes them. Or that dreams visit them at night. The Devil's work on an idle mind they would say, if I were to tell.

I rose to take leave of their women's talk and stepped out onto a trail of flat rocks that stretched across the shallow creek. Stopping at the very last one, I squatted and dropped my things into the water, swishing them back and forth absentmindedly with my fingertips. After a time, I fished around in my pockets for the soap I had brought, or what was left of it, thinking I would use it sparingly or else be out before the next supply was made, which was to be soon. How I loathed the boiling of scraps of fat, the shoveling of hearth ashes, the back-breaking, odious-smelling, day-long labor for the benefit of every unwashed body in town!

I knew this was a complaining thought and scolded myself for it. I had much to be grateful for—Father's health, plenty to eat, this day. Feeling the sun again, I rubbed the soap to the linens and took in the dark beauty of the wood. Suddenly, the dream that had taken to stealing my sleep of late seeped into my thoughts like water to a cloth.

In my dream, I cross this very creek and enter the silence of the wood. A path appears and I take it. It twists and turns in an endless tangle. I am lost. A woman stands motionless in the distance. She wears but a nightdress and her hair is down and uncovered. I open my mouth to call for help for she frightens me, but nothing comes forth. Strangled in my throat is a word. It is "Mother. Mother."

I twisted father's shirt as tightly as I could, squeezing out the last drop of water and vowing to banish such childish thoughts from my mind. I am fourteen years old and the mistress of my father's house, I told myself. I splashed water on my face, welcoming the sting of the cold and moved back over the rocks to the grass, my wet bundle dripping up my elbows and dampening my sleeves.

More goodwives had arrived in the meantime, many with small children, which brought welcome talk and laughter. I would like to have stayed and played with some of the little ones, but there were chores to be done. As I took up my buckets and yoke, I heard a low rumble in the distance, causing me to pause. Just then a gust of wind blew up, sending a chill straight through me. Certainly it was not thunder on this cloudless day, I thought. No one else took notice and I bent again to my task. As the noise began to grow, I recognized the distinct r-r-rat-tat-a-tat, r-r-rat-tat-a-tat of beating drums. Then, I heard shouting. The goodwives heard it, too, for all at once they stopped to listen. As it was not training day for the militia, I was curious as to what the commotion might be and decided to have a look for myself.

I scrambled up the embankment and walked the short distance to the end of Spring Lane where it meets the Cornhill Road. The three goodwives followed close behind. They were whispering. I tossed a look over my shoulder, but as I outpaced them, I could not make out their words— and certainly not through the roar that assaulted my ears from a fast-moving procession heading our way.

I shielded my eyes from the sun. At the head of the procession was the town crier and behind him rows of drummers. There were soldiers on horseback, too many to count, and dozens more on foot armed with muskets and pike. Scores of townsfolk followed.

"Give ear, people of Boston, rich and poor, small and great, high and low, bond or free. All of you that dwells therein," bellowed the crier.

"There she is. There's the harlot," said Goody Burrows hotly behind my ear.

"Where? Where?" I said. My eyes searched the crowd, eager to know the identity of the sinner. But all was confusion—shouting, fists waving, dust rising high in the air. The crowd moved like a thing possessed, whirling and unstoppable, and I knew then that the woman in question would be found at the center of it, like the eye of a storm. The crier confirmed it.

"…hear ye one and all. On this day William Robinson, Marmaduke Stevenson, and Mary Dyer are to be hanged until they are dead on Boston Common by order of His Excellency Governor Endicott and supported by the authority of the court, the laws of Massachusetts Bay Colony, and the law of God."

Chapter Two

The Prisoners

"Serves 'em right, them Quakers," said Goody Burrows, "especially that Dyer woman."

"Why? What did they do?" I asked.

"They consort with the Devil," she snapped. "Just look at 'em. Shameless!"

I turned to see three prisoners passing before my eyes—two men and a woman, very plain in their apparel, very grave and serious. So *this* is the heretic, the Jezebel, the Devil's harlot, I thought. And then I saw the bold thing that told me this was so. They were holding hands! She, a woman of middle years, was holding hands in public with two young men! Bolder still was the look in their eyes; all three pairs fixing straight ahead on something no one else could see. Ghoulish it was and it gave me a shiver. The crowd shouted all sorts of terrible things at them— "Blasphemers!" "Liars!" "Debauchers!"—telling them to go back to where they came from, to go back to Rhode Island, to Portsmouth Colony where they belonged.

I could not for the life of me understand how the prisoners never flinched, not even for a second. Could they not *hear* the terrible curses? Could they not see the fists raised against them? Perhaps they were heartened by the few sympathizers who, with equal feeling, begged them to repent and be spared their lives. To my mind, they appeared to be deaf to the world, deaf and dumb and blind. Suddenly, a voice from the crowd rose above the noise.

"Are ye not ashamed to walk hand in hand for all to see?"

I held my breath and looked to the woman prisoner for her reaction. She stopped and calmly turned to the speaker. Astonishingly, the entire procession stopped with her. Every soldier stood still; not a single one prodded her with his weapon. Even the drummers ceased their beat. The woman was but a few yards from me now, and I studied her closely. She was comely, small in stature, and as unlike a prisoner as I had ever seen.

"No, I am not ashamed," she answered, without a hint of fear in her voice nor modesty in her manner. "This is to me an hour of great joy. No one can see, hear, or understand the power of the Spirit which I now feel." Her eyes swept the hushed crowd and for one brief moment, they locked on mine. Ice blue they were, and they held me fast, as though offering a message. It was but a fleeting sensation, like a memory grasped and lost again, for the captain had gruffly ordered, "Drums beat on!" drowning out her words, which was surely his intention, and moving the procession onward.

Behind me, Goody Burrows clapped her hands above the heads of the little children, too happy at the colorful sight of drummers and soldiers and men on horseback to notice so vexing a thing as three condemned prisoners. Goody Burrows thought otherwise.

"Come along, everyone," she said, "we've better things to do than gawk at the sinners. You, too, Hannah!"

I watched as she and the women retreated to the spring, shaking their heads in disgust at the spectacle. I looked toward the road, then back over my shoulder again. To this day, I cannot explain why, in that instant and without a single thought of my duties or a word of explanation to anyone, I hitched up my skirts and ran from the spring. All I know is that something beckoned, and I had to follow it to Boston Common.

As it was less than a mile's walk, I thought I could be quick getting to the Commons and back again. Yet the going was not as easy as I had hoped, what with folks taken from their normal affairs to stop and gape and stare. In School House Lane young scholars pressed their noses to the inside of the schoolhouse windows, jostling one another for the best look. No doubt Mr. Woodmancy would make a good lesson of all of this law-breaking, I thought, given his well-known liking for the punishment rod. Customers spilled from shop doorways. People pointed and jeered. A woman in a fine hooded cloak put her hand to her mouth and hurried away in the other direction. It seemed to me there were few like her who looked as stricken and sad. Under his goldsmith sign, Daniel Parker spat into the dirt just as the prisoners passed by. Even kindly printer, William Price, got his nose out of his books to hurl an angry slur. I thought to turn back, but with town criers announcing the news at every corner, the procession was gaining followers by the minute, and I was swept along.

Judging by the excitement in the air, I would have thought it a festival day, had I not known better. Folks were swarming into the Commons from every which way on foot and by wagon. Men had laid down scythes and hammers. Women and children had stopped gathering hay and picking pumpkins. Faces usually grim from toil were flushed and lively. May the Lord forgive me but I was glad to be among them, free of my labors, even for just a little while, for I intended only to have a look at the proceedings and then be on my way.

Until I saw the *great elm*.

The massive tree with leaves a dazzling orange was always a beautiful sight in the autumn sun, and I never ceased to marvel at it. But on this day it was not so, for my eyes found its mightiest limb from which three nooses had been tied. They swayed lazily in the breeze as though to mock the occasion. It struck me then that the great elm looked not like a tree at all, but like something aflame with the fires of hell. My pace slowed and my spirits plummeted. With the prisoners well beyond my vision now, I began to see the faces of the people around me in the glow of this unearthly light. And what it did reveal! Excitement had turned to ugliness. People pushed and strained to get ahead of one another. Friends and neighbors whom I had known as gentlefolk made crude jokes and laughed, not from pleasure, but indecently, like wayward revelers in the night. Why were they eager to see people die? Was it madness? Were the Quakers doing the Devil's work by stirring us up? By making us act without reason, without pity?

What was I doing here?

I turned these questions over in my mind as I thought about the warnings from the ministers at Boston Church— and those from Father. Beware the Quakers, they had said. They are troublemakers. Refusing to swear allegiance to the colony. Refusing to become church members. The men wore hats in the presence of the magistrates. The women disrupted Thursday lecture, smashing bottles against the meetinghouse, running naked through the streets, bewitching people. Perhaps a spell was upon me right now, I thought. Perhaps Mary Dyer had bewitched me with her strange stare and that is why I had forgotten myself and come to this place. No wonder there were laws to rid us of such a presence. In my mind I saw the fierce blue of her eyes again and shuddered. They whipped women like her— stripped 'em to the waist and whipped them in the prison yard for any passer-by to see. Shameless they were, just as Goody Burrows had said. And the mutilations! I had heard tell about those. Tongues bored through with burning awls. The ears of more than one young man cut to the quick. First, they had been only fined for meeting and preaching, but since they continued to break the law, harsher punishments were needed. They deserved it. Everybody said so. Who but the truly wicked would risk such terrible judgment?

As much as I pondered these things, it disturbed me still to think of the dignity and beauty of this woman, Mary Dyer. How could she be dangerous? How could she be a "Jezebel"—that sinful woman from the Bible? What did such a name truly mean? Could a law really condemn a woman to *death*?

Suddenly, I heard the sound of my name.

It was Bartholomew Cheever, the blacksmith, and he smelled of rum. "Ever been to a hangin' before, Hannah?" he said. "It's quite a sight!"

This caused me considerable worry. What if Father were told of my attendance here today? He would not approve. I kept my eyes to the ground, moved quickly by the familiar faces in the crowd, and spoke to no one. I had come this far. I would go to the great elm and still have time to collect my wash and water before Father expected me home. Provided Bartholomew (whom I could not help but remember owed Father a good deal of money) kept my whereabouts to himself, Father need not know where I had been. Besides, I thought, Bartholomew might be too inebriated to recall the encounter once his wits finally returned.

I hung back a little, looking for a quiet place where I could observe away from it all. Finding a small knoll unoccupied but for a few grazing cows, I climbed to the top and looked down upon the crowd gathered about the great elm. Odd it was how almost everyone had settled into attentiveness as though awaiting an election day speech or a proclamation from the magistrates. Here and there a stray beast lumbered among the people. Children ran about in play. It all appeared so ordinary. Or so I told myself, for I knew at heart that I had let my curiosity get the better of me. Despite my misgivings about being where I did not belong, I leaned against a young birch tree and waited for something to happen.

Presently, a half-dozen men on horseback dismounted near the foot of the gallows. Distinguishable by their black caps and fine frock coats were Governor John Endicott, Deputy Governor Richard Bellingham, Assistant Simon Bradstreet, and the ministers of Boston Church, John Norton, John North, and John Wilson. I was much encouraged by the sight of Pastor Wilson who had remained atop his steed. A respected elder, a man of God, surely he would convince the Quakers to repent just as he convinced his congregation every Sunday to sin no more and walk in righteousness. I clung fast to the tree when I saw him lean down toward the prisoners to speak. "Shall such jacks as you come before authority with your hats on," I heard him say gruffly. My heart sank. This was not the manner I had hoped to hear.

The prisoner called Robinson answered. "Mind you that it is not for keeping on the hat that we are put to death," he said.

The audacious reply outraged Pastor Wilson for at once he gave an order to the marshal, who shouted an order to the guards, who roughly pulled William Robinson forward. The hangman stepped in and tied Robinson's arms behind his back. He presented the prisoner to the crowd. Many scoffed at him, but Robinson showed no fear. I thought of Pontius Pilate and Jesus and trembled.

Then Robinson spoke in a loud, clear voice, just like a preacher: "Mind you, that we are seekers of the truth. The Spirit dwells within us. This is the day the Lord has risen in his mighty power to be avenged on all his adversaries. I suffer for Christ in whom I live and for whom I die."

The real preacher, Pastor Wilson, was not moved. "Hold your tongue!" he shouted. "Be silent or else you will die with a lie in your mouth!"

The hangman came forward again and draped a cloth over Robinson's head to cover his face. He led him up the ladder and bound his legs together. Then, he slipped the rope around his neck. I can still feel the bark of the slender birch against my face and hear the gasp from the crowd. I had hidden my eyes.

Finally, slowly, I summoned the courage to uncover them. I am not certain how much time had passed, but when I looked up, the one called Marmaduke Stevenson had been readied in the same manner. He stood straight and proud—I could tell by the lift of his chin—next to the hanging body of Robinson. It was twitching. Strangely, this time, the crowd was very quiet—the same people who jeered but a moment ago. It was as though they *wanted* to hear his words, his last words.

"Be it known to all that we suffer not as evildoers but for conscience sake." These were the only words he spoke. The hangman covered his face and kicked the ladder free. The roped jerked. This time, I made myself watch. I have seen animals slaughtered before—messily and with a lot of raucous and noise, but always quickly. Yet for a man, the procedure was slow, slow and quiet.

Mary Dyer was next. My insides churned a sour taste in my mouth. I began to feel that I was foolish beyond words ever to have come. Yet, my eyes needed to find her one more time. The guards dragged her forward and presented her to the hangman. She looked up at her companions as he performed the ritual, tying her skirts around her legs and binding her arms behind her back. But there was one difference—Pastor Wilson himself offered a large handkerchief to cover her face. She said not a word while the rope was placed around her neck.

For several seconds I could hear nothing but the pounding of my heart. Beads of moisture prickled my skin even though a chill had risen in the air. I could stand it no longer. I bolted from the hill, pushing blindly through the crowd only to find myself in great peril—direct in the path of a galloping horse. Dumbstruck to the soles of my feet, I thought for all the world that I would be trampled under its pounding hooves. But Providence saved me, for the rider, though driving his mare furiously and spinning me around, missed me by a hair. Recovering, I caught the sight of him, one hand madly beating his horse with the reins and waving a scroll with the other.

He was shouting. "A reprieve! Stop! She is reprieved! Mary Dyer is reprieved from the gallows!"

Chapter Three

Reprieved

In the dusty wake of the galloping horse, I rubbed dirt from my eyes, not knowing which way to turn. People ran, shouted, tripped over one another, undoubtedly to carry the news back to their neighbors. But I began walking in the other direction, drawn back to the great elm to see for myself this baffling turn of events. Eventually, I hastened through the streaming crowd to reach the gallows, where stealing past a row of guards, I beheld a wondrous sight. Mary Dyer stood erect upon the ladder. The hangman had released her from the binding ropes and was lifting the handkerchief that covered her head. People were shouting, "Pull her down! Pull her down!" She blinked into the glare of the bright sun and a look of surprise crossed her face.

"Will," she cried, "Son!" The young man who came forward to receive her embrace was none other than the rider of the galloping horse, Mary Dyer's own son. They stood that way for several moments. Pastor Wilson turned his back on them disapprovingly and began poring over the proclamation that the young man had delivered. I had never seen Pastor Wilson's face look so red and fearsome. It would not have surprised me if he had clutched at his heart and fallen cold to the ground, for I had seen a man turn that color and die on the spot. But he stood firm, reading the scroll and frowning. Governor Endicott, wearing the cruelest of smiles, ordered Pastor Wilson to read the document aloud:

"After consideration of the petition of mercy proffered by William Dyer, her son, it is hereby ordered on authority of Governor Endicott and his Court of Assistants that Mary Dyer will be carried to the place of execution and there to stand upon the gallows with a rope about her neck, till the rest of her fellow prisoners be executed. Only until then will she be spared to be returned to prison and remain until her son or some other shall escort her out of this jurisdiction. If she is found herein after forty-eight hours, she shall be forthwith executed."

So *that* was the meaning behind the governor's cold smile, I thought. Her reprieve had been decided all along! It was to be her punishment to behold the deaths of her friends. It chilled my heart to know that she was made to watch and wait. By then I was so close to Pastor Wilson that I could almost touch his coattails as he paced back and forth. First, he huddled with the governor in a conference I could not hear. Then, taking resolute strides toward the Dyers, he roughly pulled them apart. His eyes narrowed over silver spectacles. I have often thought that Pastor Wilson has a way of looking at people, as though seeing through to the sins on their souls. From the pulpit, that look always goes to the pit of me, but Mistress Dyer appeared unmoved, which rankled him even more, for there was bitterness in his voice when he said, "What say you now, Mistress Dyer, now that the court has seen fit to grant you mercy?"

"I will stand with my brethren and suffer as they have suffered until your wicked laws are annulled," she answered.

Pastor Wilson looked about to let fly with a tongue-lashing, but Will Dyer stepped in, clasping his mother firmly by the shoulders. "I beg of you, stop this," he said, choking back tears.

This time the governor himself interceded. The bags of his eyes bulged like flour sacks and his long, narrow beard quivered like the quill of a pen as he spoke. "Mistress Dyer," he began painfully slow, "you were brought face-to-face with death this day that you might experience its chill and repent your sins. Unlike your misfortunate brethren, *you* have been given a second chance. Do not try the court's patience with your pernicious obstinacy."

Everybody knew that Governor Endicott was a hard-hearted man who would not hesitate to send a woman to the pillory or give a man twenty stripes for the slightest offense. It has been said of him that he would hang a body on Monday for killing a mouse on Sunday. He had proved his fierceness as a military commander fighting a war with the Indians. It happened many years ago but the tale remains: every Pequot man, woman, and child in sight had been slain. He brought severed limbs to Boston to celebrate the victory. So when he showed even an ounce of tolerance, I took heart, praying with all my might that Mistress Dyer would show the same in return. I desperately wanted her to repent, so that the killing would stop and all would be well again. But as I was beginning to see with my own eyes, Mary Dyer was no ordinary prisoner.

"Governor," she replied, "I come not for mercy, but for justice. I come to challenge you to change your laws which are an abomination in the sight of God."

I held my breath because the look on the governor's face told me his tolerance had run its course. "Silence!" he roared. "Take this woman away!"

The marshal clasped Mary Dyer's arm. She followed him a few steps and looked back at her son. Suddenly, her knees gave way and she crumpled to the ground. She had fainted. Whether from fear or joy or grief, I could not tell, but she was alive! Surely, God had worked His wonderful power to save her! Surely, God was on her side! I realized that I was overcome with gladness. I, Hannah Pryor, was glad for this prisoner, this lawbreaker, the Devil's harlot.

The sun hung directly overhead now. It was well past the hour when I should have been home. I had to hurry.

* * * * *

As the walk back to Plouder's Point had been long and my load from the spring heavy, I went immediately to the lean-to and filled the washbasin with water to splash my face. The cold stung the blisters on the palms of my hands, which were trembling slightly. I patted them dry on my skirt, tucked several stray pieces of hair into my cap, and took a deep breath. Then, I went into the kitchen to tend the noontime meal, which I had left simmering in the kettle. The hearth embers were barely warm and I had to poke them with an iron and blow until they glowed red so that I could add a few more sticks. I tested the meat, turnips, and cabbage; they had cooled, but they were cooked sufficiently. There was enough time to warm the pot some before Father entered. In the meantime, I folded the clean linens, swept the floor, chasing a little mouse back into its hole, laid the board, and waited for him.

My heart took a small leap when I heard the door of the carpentry shed slam shut. I suppose I felt jittery because I intended not to tell him where I had been. He would not have approved of my leaving my chores and certainly not of attending a hanging. In Father's mind the witnessing of a public execution was not for sport or merriment as some people would have it, nor was it suitable for a girl. As to why I had gone and why I had stayed I had no explanation, not even to myself. It was best, I reckoned, to go about as usual. Yet, when Father entered the kitchen, my voice conveyed a brightness that I did not truly feel. Happily for me, he did not seem to notice and took his place at the head of the board in his ordinary, quiet way. I ladled out a large bowl for him and a small one for myself. He bowed his head, mumbled thanks to the Lord, and dug in hungrily. For some reason, as I took my own place, I felt a pang of loneliness. A board such as this should have a large, noisy family around it. I watched Father out of the corner of my eye while he ate. Flecks of sawdust adorned his greying beard and I felt an urge to brush them away like I used to do when I was a little girl. But that would be a silly thing to do now. He would think so, too.

Normally at our noontime meal, I would entertain Father with talk of who might have passed by on the road that day, what mischief our little goats were up to, or some such thing. He would laugh and smile or tell a story of his own, if he had been to town that morning. Lately, though, his stories were few and his manner sullen. I sensed that the business of the colony—now that he was to stand for election to the General Court—pressed heavily upon him. What with more and more settlers arriving all the time, land to be distributed, disputes settled, and now the Quaker trouble, it was no wonder. His mind burdened thus put him at a distance from me, and it had been this way for some weeks. I was surprised then that he missed my chatter, because after a time, he looked up and said, "You're awful quiet, daughter. You're not ailing, are ye?"

"No, Father," I said.

"Good, because I slaughtered a pig this morning. The innards are in the dairy house. You'd best get them on to boil soon."

In my mind's eye appeared the lifeless bodies of William Robinson and Marmaduke Stevenson. That sour taste rose again in my throat.

"And the flitches of bacon are standin' in the salt. You'll be sure to hang them in the chimney within the fortnight, won't you? We don't want to be without meat this winter."

I looked away, putting a hand to my mouth.

"Hannah, are ye certain you're not ailing? You look terrible sick."

I assured him that I was well and rose to pour him a cup of cider from the barrel, thinking that by moving about I'd put some color back into my cheeks—and that he'd stop talking about the slaughtered pig.

I returned with the cider and sat down. When the queasiness had passed, I felt strong enough to venture a question that was on my mind, for Father was always a willing teacher with a way of explaining that made clear many a difficult thing.

"They hanged some people on the Commons today," I began, matter of factly. "I saw the prisoners and guard pass by when I was at the spring. They were Quakers."

"Aye, daughter, I know."

"Why did they hang them? I do not truly understand the crime."

He chewed his food thoughtfully for several moments before he answered. "They flaunt the laws of God and the laws of the Commonwealth. They want to weaken our community. They are rightly punished." He reached for the bread and cut himself a generous slice with his pocketknife.

I felt not at all satisfied with the explanation and ventured another question. "How so? How do they weaken our community?"

"They turn us against ourselves by questioning the wisdom of our elders."

"Cannot the elders use their wisdom to make them see differently?" I asked.

"It is thanks to the elders' wisdom that laws have been enacted to make them see differently."

"Yet these Quakers today were unmoved by the harshest law of them all—death!"

He sighed. "Do not imitate their blasphemy with questioning of your own."

I chewed on my lip a bit, mulling this over. "By blasphemy do you mean how they refuse to swear allegiance or go to meeting?"

"Aye, that's right."

"Is there such harm in this that they deserve to die?"

"Oh, child, there is harm, indeed. They do not conform. They wish to destroy this colony and all that we have worked so hard to build. That is their crime, and mind you, it is a serious one."

"But they seem to be peaceable, Father."

"That is an illusion."

"People cursed and spat at them and they did not retaliate."

"They will retaliate in their own time, in their own way."

"But they say the Spirit is within them. Does that not mean they are godly people?"

"Have you not been listening to Pastor Wilson? Quakers put themselves above the law of man and they sin against the law of God. They are an abomination."

"What about mercy, Father? What about Christian charity?"

"There can be no mercy or Christian charity without first there being unity and stability," he said, his voice rising. "*They* choose chaos and lawlessness."

I pressed on. "But Mistress Dyer...she seems gentle and kind..."

His face reddened. "The Devil takes many forms," he snapped.

"Oh, Father," I couldn't help but blurt out, "surely the Devil cannot reside in someone so forthright!"

He answered me with a storm in his grey eyes.

I tried to sound more reasonable. "It is simply that Mistress Dyer has neither the tongue nor appearance of wickedness."

He threw down his spoon with a force that made me jump. "Do not speak that woman's name ever again in this house," he said, with a finger pointed in warning.

I was stunned into silence. Father had never spoken to me with such harshness before. I felt bewildered and hurt, not quite knowing what had I done wrong. The hurt, however, quickly turned to guilt because I felt myself to blame. Should I admit having followed the Quakers to the Commons? Better to confess now than to suffer the consequences of having deceived if he should find out, but fear kept me speechless and rooted to my seat.

Minutes passed ever so slowly as we finished our meal. I ate but a few bites, food having no taste for me, and kept silent with my eyes down so as not to cause further disturbance. When Father finally rose, I stiffened in anticipation of what he would say, but he merely paused, running a hand through his hair, and turned to go. At the door, grabbing his hat, he said, "I will want you with me tomorrow at market, daughter. So be quick about your chores today." His tone was gentler now, and I knew he was sorry for the bad temper, though he would never say as much. I simply could not understand how the mention of this woman's name could anger him so.

Chapter Four

Scandal Close to Home

I woke the next day before the light. It took a full moment to realize I was in my own bed in my own house, for I had awakened from a terrible dream, a different dream from the one that had been coming to me of late. I recalled it vividly. I was being dragged and pulled through the streets by a fearsome mob. People with twisted faces threw mud and rocks at me. With all my might I tried to break free but could not. The weight of bodies pressed on all sides. I felt surely I would suffocate. There was a tree. Beside it stood Father. He was putting a rope around Mary Dyer's neck. That's when I awoke. Fumbling for my clothes in the dark, I dressed quickly, and descended the ladder to the kitchen, wishing day would soon break.

Father had already risen and gone to his shed. I should be ashamed to say it, but I was glad to be alone. We had spent the previous evening in silence; he to his Bible, and I to writing in my daybook and to ponder my recent misdeeds—leaving my chores, putting myself in the presence of the Quakers, angering Father with my incessant questions, allowing yet another dream to addle my thoughts. I resolved to do better on this new day. And so I went lively about my tasks. I milked the goats, fed the chickens and pigs, and gave the hearth a good sweeping out. I even managed to get the boiled innards over to Goody

Colburn's house, so she would make them into the smoked links that Father enjoyed so much. I sang softly to myself for good cheer and prayed for divine guidance and salvation. All the while, though, another part of me wished to crawl back under my warm, heavy bedclothes, where I could sleep without dreaming, where I could be free of this qualmy feeling in the pit of my belly.

I knew that if anything could brighten my dark spirits, market day could. The air was unseasonably warm and dry with only a few wispy clouds in the sky as Father and I set out for town, the wagon packed to overflowing with wainscot chairs, stools, cabinets, and a drop-leaf table. More than once I had to rescue a piece from falling out, for despite the tying of ropes, the wagon dipped and swayed in and out of ruts so deep, I feared falling out myself. I gripped the sides fast and hung on tight, turning my head this way and that all along the Middle Road to see who might be coming to market that day. I must have made an amusing sight, for I could see a smile lift a corner of Father's mouth.

We crossed the bridge at Mill Creek where the water turns the great wheels of the grist mills. Beyond the mills came the sounds of the North End's boatyards where shipwrights, caulkers, rope workers, and blacksmiths labored noisily over pinnaces, ketches, yawls, and full-rigged ships to rival those made in England. Father had taught me how to tell one boat from the other. I loved to call out their names as we passed the wharves at Bendell's Cove.

"Do you see over there?" said Father, motioning with his reins.

I shielded my eyes toward Town Dock and the great bay that stretched far into the distance.

"It's the *Rose 'n Thorn*. She sailed from England to Barbados to Boston and is bound again for home."

I had never before seen such a magnificent sailing vessel. It was the tallest one in the bay.

"She's beautiful," I said, imagining the sight of her massive sails unfurled and billowing in the wind, imagining what grand adventures awaited her crew, imagining just how blue was the blue of the West Indies water I had been told of. They say that people swim in it.

"The ship's master will likely be at market today to buy goods to sell back in England. I expect that trade will be brisk. It's also likely he'll have brought over some new settlers in need of furnishin' a home."

Perhaps it was simply the prospect of customers that made Father's spirits rise, but I smiled, anyway, happy to have lightness between us once again.

"He'll be *selling* cargo, too, from England as well as the West Indies."

"Slaves, Father?" I asked. "Do you think his cargo includes slaves?" It was but last spring, when we had gone to Town Dock to deliver some of Father's work to an English traveler, that I had watched the sale of a family of Negroes. There, in the middle of the dock, the captain haggled with the buyer over their price as though they were oxen or steer. My mind's eye recalled the solemn black faces, a little girl among them, no older than six years, holding a poppet, like one I had had as a child. I remembered, too, the thin clothing, impossibly protective against the cold, wet wind of a New England March. I never saw them again in the town and often wondered what had become of them.

"The demand for servants grows as our colonies grow," answered Father. "One thing the *Rose 'n Thorn* is certain to have," he said, changing the topic, "spices!" There was a glimmer in his eye.

"May I purchase some molasses and sugar, then?"

"First, let's see how well our own trade goes before we start spendin' profits we don't have."

I assured him that I just knew he would have many good customers.

"God willing," he said.

"God willing," I repeated, hoping the *Rose 'n Thorn* would not have brought slave children to sell at market today.

Father steered the wagon into the square. Up ahead the ground floor of Keane's Town House overflowed with bushel upon bushel of grain, apples, Indian corn, pumpkins, squash, parsnips, dried herbs, and cabbages. I marveled at the bountiful harvest that God had granted us. And I brightened at the hum of noise from townfolk, countryfolk, new settlers, Indians, and rough-looking mariners. Herdboys drove sheep with long sticks. Geese tried to flee their owners. Cows, pigs, and chickens were there in abundance as were household goods to dazzle many a mistress—holland board-cloth edged with lace, brass candlesticks, chaffing dishes, turkey carpets, chintz quilts, English-made clocks and watches that go eight or nine days without winding up.

Father found a place for the wagon between Joshua Grafton and his salt cod and Samuel Plummer and his pewter wares. Even though Joshua's fish barrel stank to the high heavens, I hardly minded because he told the best seafaring stories about shipwrecks and mutinies and man-eating sharks. I never really knew which parts were true and which were fancy, but he usually gave us a piece of salt cod at the end of the day. Father said that it was for putting up with his tall tales. And Samuel Plummer always had a kind word for me. Now and again he would give me a real shilling coin just for polishing up a mug or a plate, which I would have done for nothing at all, so pretty they were. One day I would buy a handsome platter for Father and me.

Once settled, I sat on a stool to await the customers, calling out greetings to passers-by I knew while Father talked with Sam and Joshua about business matters. My ears pricked up, however, when I heard someone say the word "Quaker." Pretending to busy myself with the ledger, I listened.

"Nasty business, yesterday," said Joshua from behind his fish barrels. "What say you about it, Jonah?"

"Unfortunate, but necessary," was Father's reply.

"Say what you will about the Quakers," said Sam looking about him suspiciously before he finished speaking his mind, "I don't hold with killin' a woman. It ain't right."

"I might remind you, Sam, that she is quite alive," returned Father.

"Well, they came mighty close to seeing that she wasn't, now didn't they," he replied, muttering something else under his breath about Governor Endicott being a bloodthirsty something or other. Sam was known for saying he'd sooner hear a cat meow than Pastor Wilson speak. I was glad when he lowered his voice because one had to be very careful; speaking against an elder could put a man in the stocks. I did not want to see that happen to Sam.

Father steered the topic in another direction. "We must not let ourselves be distracted from our true purpose— that of making this colony strong and godly and prosperous."

"If you ask me, the magistrates care more about the prosperity of England than they do about hard-working farmers and merchants this side of the sea," said Joshua. Joshua could also be vocal about matters especially when it came to the magistrates' fixing prices to benefit English buyers.

"Aye, that's where our attention should be," said Father.

"What's that you say, Jonah?" asked the old fisherman, leaning an elbow on a barrel top. "Maybe you're ready to go along with the rest of us in a petition to lift restrictions on prices!" Joshua, seeing me eavesdropping, gave me a wink of a very blue eye on a very crinkled face.

"Change must come slowly and from them that knows best, not from petitions," said Father.

"Well, Jonah, looks like we'll just have to wait 'til *you're* elected for things to change!"

"If it's God's will and for the common good, things will change," said Father.

"You're a just man, Jonah Pryor. That's why I'll cast my ballot for ye, my boy, in the spring election. We could use more deputies like you," said Joshua wrapping up a piece of salt cod for a customer, who as it turns out, was Merry Winslow, brimming with tidings for me.

"Hannah, you won't believe it," she gushed. Her fair curls bounced as she ran toward me.

"We went to the hangings yesterday! Mother and I!"

I quickly took her elbow and led her a few feet away so that Father could not hear. Merry kept chattering freely.

"I know it's vulgar," she said, "but we simply had to be there. Mother had heard through Papa's connections that there was going to be a surprise waiting for that Quaker woman. A surprise she'd never forget!"

"The reprieve, you mean."

"Of course! Everybody's talking about it. That and the turning off of those other two. You should have heard them in the tavern. Folks were falling all over one another trying to come up with the goriest details."

"Yes, I know about it," was all I could share with her for the moment.

Merry continued. "Then, as we were coming out the door, along comes crazy Jane Hawkins, saying over and over, 'Try as you might, she will not die.'"

"Who will not die?" I asked.

"Mistress Dyer, of course, you ninny!"

"Hush," I said, noticing that Father was watching us out of the corner of his eye. "What did she mean by that?"

"Oh, it's just gibber-jabber! Nobody pays that old beggar woman any heed. I told her to hold her tongue or they'd come for her, too!" Merry laughed.

"Merry, really, you *can* be unkind."

"Want to know something else?"

"What?"

"Mother says that Jane Hawkins was a midwife to Mary Dyer and people say that that's what made her go squirrelly in the head."

"Jane Hawkins, a midwife to Mary Dyer?"

"More than once. She had a whole brood of babies."

"Mary Dyer lived here in Boston?"

"A long time ago. Until they forced her out. Some kind of scandal."

"What scandal?"

"I don't know. I've been trying to wriggle it out of Mother, but she tells me she prefers not to put wicked thoughts in my head. She says I have enough of them on my own."

A scandal. The mere word gave me a shiver.

"Ask your father, Hannah. The Dyers were among the first settlers to arrive. I should think he knew them."

"Was she forced out because she was a Quaker?" I asked.

"Mother says she only became a Quaker when she went to England a few years ago. Left behind her husband and children—one of them a newborn. Nobody quite knows what happened to her over there but she stayed a long time. Mother says she's a queer one. As queer as Jane Hawkins."

"How does your mother come to know this?"

"I don't know. Everybody loves a good scandal. It's just that respectable people don't talk about it...except in a whispery kind of way."

What kind of woman would leave a newborn child to sail across the ocean, I thought.

"Why are you curious about Mary Dyer, anyway, Hannah? Aren't you afraid she's a witch?" Merry, who never took a thing too seriously, made a devilish face to tease me.

I thought about her question a moment because I was not at all sure of the answer. And then it occurred to me. What I feared most was not that Mary Dyer was a witch, but that she wasn't a witch at all.

Chapter Five

The Letter

A letter arrived by the hand of our neighbor Jonathan Tishmond that set my heart in a flutter. It was from London. Jonathan had just ridden in from Town Dock and was full of news from an English brig called the *Wanderer*. Nary a word did I hear him utter, for my thoughts were only for this letter. Its feminine hand and noble seal meant it could be from one person only—my aunt, my mother's sister. What news did it carry? About the estate? About her health? Was she coming to New England? Father being away at the training field for militia exercises, I would have to wait for his return to find out, for the letter was addressed to him. Oh, how long the wait would be, I thought, knowing I need muster a great deal of patience, as it was unlikely he would return before nightfall. I thought it best to busy myself in the garden just to put the letter—and temptation—out of sight.

Mother had started the garden many years ago. She had tilled the soil, built the beds, and searched for rocks of even size and color to trim the edges of each of the four plots—two for flowers and two for herbs. A proper English garden. Something she had insisted on having once her new home at Plouder's Point was completed. Or so Father had told me once a long time ago. There was even a row of buttonwood trees at the garden's back, just like at the governor's house.

Father had tended the garden until I was old enough to do it myself. It was Goody Burrows, though, who had taught me to plant columbine and foxglove, feverfew and winter savory. How to dry them on the rafters—thyme and marjoram to flavor soups, lavender to fragrance the linens, and bayberries for candles to sweeten the air. I discarded a few stray pebbles and tried to imagine my mother working in this same spot, a young wife, not too many years older than myself. How had she managed? How had she felt about leaving behind her splendid life in England only to be consigned to a wilderness with but meager shelter for protection, wolves grinning at the edge of the wood, savages—she must have been very strong, stronger than I am. I made circles in the soil with my fingers, loosening the fine dry stuff to powder, which promptly blew away in the wind. If only there had been an herb powerful enough to save her. But there was no such thing. Women died in childbirth. It was God's will. It was God's will that she die and I be born. I picked the last herbs of the season, dropped them into my apron, and went inside.

With the herbs to dry and bread to bake, I had safely put the letter out of my mind. Morning passed quickly into afternoon and before I knew it, the sun was beginning to wane, leaving a length of shadow on the wall that told me it was time to prepare supper. I decided to make pottage from the broth of yesterday's dinner with lots of oatmeal to thicken it. I did so hastily, so that with my chores completed at least until milking, I could snatch a few moments to call my own.

Recently, Nellie Colburn had made me a blouse of linen spun from her loom. A fine blouse it was, perhaps the finest I had ever had. All it needed was a touch of embroidery to make it truly so. Not that I was skilled in the practice, but having watched Nellie's dexterous fingers make intricate patterns, I wanted to do likewise and I knew exactly what I wanted to create.

In a large trunk in the corner of the kitchen underneath a woolen blanket lay a satin ballgown. It was my mother's, worn in the days before her marriage. She must have treasured it dearly, for she had packed it among the few things allowed her for the ocean crossing in a cramped, crowded ship. It is one of a handful of her possessions that still remain—that, a book of *Sonnets* by William Shakespeare, and a silver-handled lookinglass. I know it sounds silly, but sometimes when I am low, I go to the trunk and reach inside just to touch them. I run the satin over my cheek. I trace the glass' silverwork with my fingertips. When I was very small, I would play with them, pretending I was a princess at a ball, the very ball that Mother had attended in this very dress at the palace of King Charles I. Father told me this so long ago, that I sometimes wonder if it is really true or only in my mind's fancy.

I unfolded the dress carefully, my eyes falling over the many-colored butterflies, flowers and grasshoppers that adorned it. This seamstress had worked magic even greater than Nellie Colburn's. It was the butterfly I wanted to copy even though I had no thread worthy of the original. The colors in my sewing box would have to do—saffron for gold, ash for silver, and a touch of indigo and chestnut. It would be unseemly if I were to embroider too extravagantly.

I set to work by the light of the hearth. It was difficult going. My fingers felt clumsy and the stitches were uneven. More than one needle prick nearly ruined the blouse for the blood it drew. I threaded and unthreaded and tried a smaller needle, keeping to the task until my eyes grew weary. Under good light, the handiwork looked more like a beetle than a butterfly. Or a plain, old-speckled egg. Discouraged, I folded the blouse and the gown and returned them to the trunk, then sat down in Father's chair to rest. I listened to the crackling of the fire and felt the warmth on my toes through the well-worn leather of my shoes. After a time I must have dozed, for my head dropped and I sat up with a start, only to have my eyes find the letter on the mantel. The seal had come partially undone from the heat of the fire. I listened for Father in the yard or the lean-to, but all was quiet. Oh, the temptation! The tug of curiosity! I felt its power as real as the hot rush from the hearth. I jumped up, took the letter, and carefully undid what was left of the seal with the tip of my fingernail. This is what I read:

London, August 1659.

I sincerely hope that this letter finds you and your daughter in safety and good health after so many years since our last sorrowful exchange of letters upon the death of my dearest sister, Elizabeth. The circumstances prior to her death, which were the cause of great pain and consternation, urged me then as I do now to wish you to spare your daughter any such political trials. Tidings of awful persecutions have reached these shores. I fear for Hannah if she is to follow in her mother's footsteps. Indeed, there is much to fear in the primitive New World, while in London we eagerly await the return to the throne of our dear King Charles II. Better days await us, and Hannah, if you would send her to me. She shall be given a proper education, and if she chooses to stay, a fine house and husband will be hers when she shall be of age. I begg of you to think on it as I had your word so many years ago that it would be in your consideration in God's good time. 'Tis true, I cannot but expect your distaste of it being a loving father, yet my heartfelt desire for the prosperity and happiness of my dear sister's daughter forces me to tender my acknowledgments.

I prayse God that we here are in Health, and
goe cheerfully in our businesse. May God safely
deliver this letter, and yours, against the calamities
of the sea. May He see fit that you send the words
that shall be the comfort of my life.

> Your honored sister-in-law,
> Lady Rebecca Waldron

I dropped the letter to my lap. *I fear for Hannah if she
is to follow in her mother's footsteps...if you would send
her to me...A proper education...A fine house and husband
will be hers.* I took the letter up again and reread these
words trying to take in their full meaning. Leave my home?
Leave Father? I knew not what to make of it!

Just then I heard the steady thud of Challenger's
hooves. Father had returned. Quickly, I folded the letter
and pressed the seal as hard as I could. When he entered,
I wasted no time in telling him about its arrival. A letter all
the way from England was an important event for anybody,
and a look of surprise crossed his face as he took it up. I
studied his expression as he read; his brows were knit; his
beard crackled as he scratched the skin underneath. When
he was finished, he simply folded the letter and placed it
inside his pocket without further ado.

"Well, Father," I asked, expectantly.

"From your aunt. Some business about your mother's
estate," he said waving me off. "She sends her love." He
went to the hearth, rubbing his hands over the steam from
the kettle, his eyes looking blankly toward its bottom.

"Did the exercises go well, Father?" I asked, trying to
sound unconcerned. Perhaps he needed a few moments
to collect his thoughts before he spoke about these
unsettling matters.

"Aye, indeed," he said distractedly. "The captain from
the *Wanderer* tells us that pirates have been running ships
from the Bahamas to Nova Scotia."

In truth, I was not nearly as frightened of pirates as I was of Aunt Rebecca's message.

"Not to worry," he said. "We'll keep showing our might at Fort Hill and our shores will be protected."

"I will not worry, Father," I replied.

The furrow had returned to his brow as we ate our meal in silence. After a time, I decided that perhaps he needed some gentle prodding.

"I got to thinking about England today...with the letter arriving and all. It reminded me of the story you used to tell. Mother's attendance at the king's ball. Do tell me again, Father. It has been so long since I have heard it."

"For what purpose?" he asked suspiciously.

"I...just to remember, is all," I stammered.

"That was child's play then."

I began to lose heart. The last thing I wanted was to anger Father again, so I said as gaily as I could, "I wish to hear of things beautiful and grand—"

"Of things sinful and vainglorious, you mean," he said harshly.

I was stung. I seemed always to be saying the wrong thing.

"You are no longer a child, Hannah, and should not seek childish entertainments."

"I only wish to know about life in England...Mother's life..."

"I do not wish to speak of England and its corruptions."

"Why, of course, Father, it is only that I—"

"I took your mother from that place long ago to do God's work here."

"Yes, Father."

"Let us speak no more about it."

When he finally looked upon me again, it was a softer look, yet the hurt was done. Although tears stung my eyes, I would not let him see. I rose to clear the board while he went to the mantel for the Bible and the night's reading. He sat down heavily in his chair. His rough thumb chafed against the well-worn pages with an irritating sound. After I had rinsed the bowls, I took my place beside him on the stool by the hearth. I had done this gladly nearly every evening since I can remember. He had taught me to read Scripture at an early age, delighted by my ability to recite many passages by heart. This night, however, I put my chin in my hand. It is a wicked thing to say but my heart was a stone, and I vowed to be unmoved and untouched by the power of the holy book. Even as he began to read, my thoughts were only on the wound that I nursed. When he finished reciting, he opened to the story of Abraham and held out the book to me. I took it into my lap, shifted uncomfortably on my stool, and began to read. At the meaning of the words, the stone began to soften, for the holy book has power over all hearts and minds. It spoke to me powerful, telling me to consider the terrible torments Abraham suffered as a test of his love for God. And when I recited the words describing the awful moment when Abraham raises his hand to kill his only son in sacrifice, I began to feel remorse for my own self-pity and for my disobedient ways. How can I be good, I thought. How can I be good so that Father does not send me away?

I handed the Bible back to him for the last reading of the night. He chose Proverbs 31, the story of Bathsheba, and read these words:

> She looketh well to the way of her household,
>   and eateth not of the bread of idleness.
> Her children arise up and call her blessed; her
>   husband also, and he praiseth her.
> Many daughters have done virtuously, but thou
>   excellest them all.
> Favor is deceitful, and beauty is vain: but a
>   woman that fearest the Lord, she shall be praised.

Give her of the fruit of her hands; and let her own
works praise her in the gates.

Afterwards, I watched Father staring into the fire as I
climbed the ladder to the loft. His figure cast a gigantic,
brooding shadow on the rough clay wall. As I undressed
quickly and got into bed, my mind was a swirl of questions.
What was he thinking? Was there a message to me in the
Proverb about being a "virtuous" daughter? Why did he
not "praise his wife" and call her "blessed"? What did Aunt's
letter mean? Had Mother done something wrong? Was it
akin to the reason they nearly hanged Mary Dyer? Is that
why Father forbid that her name be spoken? And what
about the "scandal"? Just what kind of disgrace had driven
her away?

Most of all, with the arrival of the letter, what was to
become of *me*?

One thing was certain. If the answers would not come
from Father, I knew of one person whom I could ask.

Chapter Six

Goody Hawkins

All that I knew about Jane Hawkins was that she was very poor and lived alone in a mud-walled cottage along an Indian path just beyond Roxbury Neck. Ever since I can remember folks had called her a witch. I always supposed this to be true since she dressed in ragged clothes and had a sour smell about her. Yet at market, where the worse she would do was beg for food and make annoyances with her loud talk to no one in particular, she seemed harmless enough. She never brought calamity to anyone as far as I reckoned.

Deeming it a good three miles to Goody Hawkins' cottage, I knew I could be back in as many hours. Perhaps, I might even chance to see her on the Cornhill Road and save myself the long walk to Roxbury Village. For what I desired was but a few minutes with her where none could watch and listen, where I could ask questions freely. If an elder were to hear me speaking of Mistress Dyer with the likes of Jane Hawkins, I should fear the consequences. More than once I told myself that the whole idea was foolhardy. Goody Hawkins might chase me away or speak in a strange tongue like witches were wont to do, or worse, cause me violence. Still, I was not swayed. Whatever force had pressed me onward the day of the hangings was at work on me now. I had to go. I decided to bring a loaf of bread hoping she would find the gesture neighborly-like and be kind to me.

Upon reaching town square, I turned into Prison Lane. As good fortune would have it, the whipping posts and stocks were empty of transgressors. When they were not, when some man or woman was tied to the post, or held fast by the neck and wrists in the tight grip of the stocks, I would do what I could to avoid the sight. They may have been thieves and drunkards, but it distressed me to see them at the mercy of boys throwing mud and grown people laughing and jeering. That day, however, I wished to pass the prison directly because it was there that Mary Dyer had been taken after her reprieve.

As I approached, Governor Endicott and Deputy Governor Bellingham emerged from the prison door. I lowered my eyes and tried to make myself small in their presence, being as they were important men. While I walked quietly behind them, I heard this exchange:

"Thankfully, the woman is well on her way to Rhode Island," said Richard Bellingham.

"And none too soon," said the governor. "By my word, had the protests continued, none would be spared the lash!"

"Now that she be gone, things will be right again."

"We shall take no chances. Keep the ropes in plain sight for all to take example from."

We parted ways at the Cornhill Road, although they seemed to have taken no notice of me all the while. As I left the prison behind, I wished Mary Dyer God's grace on her journey in words uttered underneath my breath. Providence had made us fellow travelers on this day. Though our destinations were different, I fancied myself like her, a "seeker" of truth. Happy to know that she was safely bound for home, I moved briskly onward in order to make good time.

The day was clear and the walking pleasant even across Roxbury Neck where the wind off the sea is known to blow terrible. In Roxbury Village, a farmer and his family stopped to offer a ride in their wagon, but I waved them on, preferring not to reveal my destination. Doubtless, the farmer would not have approved of my taking the Indian path alone. Settlers were forever wary of girls or women being taken captive. I was not afraid. Indian runners carrying messages from one English village to another were common, and I had never heard tell of even one of them causing a person harm. In truth, what I feared was the forest itself and the woman in my dream. The thought that she might be waiting for me filled me with dread, but I pushed it quickly from my mind when I saw the path I needed to take up ahead.

I knew which one it was for it was marked by an unusual sign—a large rock in the shape of a toad—a giant, sloe-eyed toad. At least that is what my memory told me. I was but a child the first time I saw it, learning that it marked where Goody Hawkins lived. The way I recall it, Father and I were returning from picking corn in his field when we happened upon the old woman on a road just outside of town square. She appeared to be heading home, empty-handed of any charitable gift a person might fain to give. Out of pity, for I knew that is how he felt, Father offered her a ride in his wagon. What is striking in my memory is how she seemed to talk familiarly with Father and he with her—this woman whom most people shunned. I have no recollection as to what words passed between them, yet even now I can recall the feeling of surprise it gave me. We left her at the start of this very path, my childish mind believing the toad to be a sign of Goody Hawkins' witchcraft.

As I stood before it again, the toadlike stone looked so like the witch's sign I remembered that I had to touch it just to reassure myself of its lifelessness. Its cold hardness told me it was but a great ordinary rock, whereupon I took my first steps onto the path that would take me to Goody Hawkins' cottage.

Dry twigs cracked beneath my feet as I walked the narrow, worn trail. A hawk screamed overhead. I looked up, but could not see it through the thickness of the tall pines that stood like sentries guarding against the light. Here and there, however, great beams were able to break through, and I ran from one to the next, as in a game, to keep from fright. Soon, all was silent except for the whispering of those pines, and my footsteps muffled by a soft, needle-strewn floor. Only once was I truly startled when a deer leapt out from behind a thicket followed by her young. I laughed to myself to wonder who was the more surprised.

Picking up my steps, I continued on for another half mile, unable to keep myself from believing that around each new bend, behind every rock or tree, the woman in the nightdress with her hair down might be waiting for me. That is why I was greatly heartened to see a thin ribbon of smoke rising above the treetops. I thanked the Lord for delivering me without incident, for I was certain that the smoke signaled my destination. Spying the cottage through the trees, however, an eerie feeling crept over me. I could turn and run without being seen, I thought. I looked back over my shoulder along the path, and finding myself not eager to return just yet, I approached the cottage, raised a fist to the decrepit door, and knocked.

I held my breath as the door slowly opened. It was Jane Hawkins.

She greeted me with a squinted eye and a "Come in, dearie," as though she had expected me all along. The cottage was but a single room, windowless, the only light from the glow of a blaze in a tiny hearth, its smoke rising through a hole in the roof, just as in an Indian hut. The room smelled of damp fur and tobacco. I took a few steps inside onto a hard, dirt floor, my eyes combing the place for signs of witchcraft or danger. Suddenly, I caught something in the corner that caused me to flinch. It was an Indian squaw with a baby at her breast. I know I must have looked alarmed, but the squaw merely gazed back with steady, alert eyes on her otherwise expressionless face; her only movement a gentle stroke of her finger along the infant's fine black hair.

"My visitors are few," said Goody Hawkins, motioning to a stool. "Did you lose your way? Are you in need of water?"

"Why, no," I replied. I held out the bread, which I had wrapped in a cloth. She took it into her aged hands with care, turned to the squaw, said something in the Indian tongue, and laid the bread on a soot-covered board. Then, she sat down slowly in a surprisingly fine old wainscot chair. I had never been in a homey surrounding with an Indian before, nor someone who could very well be a witch. That and the awkward silence as she studied my face with one good eye—the other had a cloudiness that made it appear blind—made me squirm.

Finally, she spoke. "You're the Pryor girl, are ye not?"

"Yes," I said with surprise, since I had not spoken to the woman in so many years.

"I never forget a newborn babe," she said. "I can see its future the moment I hold it." She folded her arms across her thin chest and laughed, showing jagged toothless gums.

She speaks nonsense, I thought. I should not have come. I have made a grievous error.

"Like that babe," she continued, pointing to the squaw's small bundle. "He will be a great warrior, and the English will fear him. Mark my words, in years to come, the English will tremble for all they have done to his people."

I looked at the squaw who continued to stare at me.

"But *you* aren't to be feared, dearie, are you," said Goody Hawkins. "You're just as scrawny as the day you were born!" She laughed again, a course laugh. Then, very ordinary-like, she asked if I would like a strong hot drink.

The hospitable offer softened my misgivings somewhat, for it seemed as genuine as that of any goodwife. I managed a "yes, please," as she reached for a small battered pot on the fire.

"Is someone sick, child?" she asked, settling back into her chair. "Is the bread in payment for remedies?"

"No," I said, seeing my chance to explain my presence, "although I am told that you were once a midwife."

She handed me a small wooden bowl filled to the brim with a black liquid. The steam warmed my face as I inhaled it. It smelled of raspberry and sage. I took but a small sip, for though the room was damp, and I desired the warmth, I could not be sure it held no evil ingredients.

"Still a midwife to them that needs me." She nodded in the direction of the squaw.

"A midwife to Mary Dyer, the Quaker woman?" I asked.

"Aye," she said suspiciously. "Many years ago."

"There is something I wish to know about her. That is why I am here. I wondered if you might help." I tried to smile and act natural, but my lips trembled as I spoke.

"Why me, dearie?" She smirked, seeming to enjoy my discomfort.

"Folks say so little about her."

"*Respectable* folks is what you mean."

I lowered my eyes.

"No matter, dearie. What is it you wish to know?"

"Was she a godly woman?" I asked, looking direct upon her now.

Goody Hawkins turned down the corners of her mouth. "Strange question to be askin'! Seems the answer is as plain as the nose on your face. She'll swing from a rope one of these days. Doesn't that tell ye something?"

I made no reply.

She took a leather pouch and clay pipe from deep inside her pocket, slowly stuffed the pipe with the tobacco, touched it with a stick from the fire, and pulled on it with her sunken lips until it lit. Smoke encircled her head. I breathed in the aroma, which was not at all unpleasant.

"If it's a story you want, I'll tell ye, but it ain't pretty."

She reached forward to toss more kindling on the fire. I clasped the bowl and brought it to my chest to ward off the chill. I glanced back at the Indian squaw. The infant was fast asleep while its mother appeared to be listening as though she understood every single word.

Chapter Seven

Anne Hutchinson

"It was back some twenty years now, in the year sixteen hundred and thirty-six," said Goody Hawkins, "when the trouble began. And I can tell you who started it all. Not your Mary Dyer, but one Anne Hutchinson. Ever heard tell of her?"

I shook my head no.

"A stately, handsome woman she was, bold as brass with opinions as high and mighty as a deacon in a pulpit. Fourteen children, all told, had she and her husband, William. Now there was a cuckold if I ever saw one! Never did learn how to keep a wife quiet. And Mistress Hutchinson! What noise she made about things that were none of her business! Like Scripture. She knew the Bible inside and out as well as any minister; some said better. I'd hear her talkin' at the spring. She'd be preachin' to the womenfolk about the Sunday sermon. I never paid no heed. But many did—Mary Dyer especially—and Elizabeth Pryor.

"Mother? My mother knew Mistress Dyer?" I interrupted excitedly.

"Why, everybody knew everybody—and everybody's business. We were 'knit together as one,'" she said mockingly, "as old Governor Winthrop was fond of sayin'. Too tight, if you want my opinion."

"Was my mother a Quaker?" I asked impatiently.

"I never knew a child with so many questions!"

"Sorry," I said, biting my lip.

"Mistress Hutchinson started holdin' Scripture meetin's in her home. 'Gossipings,' the elders called 'em. They didn't approve at all, especially when more and more womenfolk started attendin'—fifty, sixty at a time. They warned her to stop. You see, they didn't take to a woman doin' a minister's job. Didn't like her interpretations of the Scripture, neither."

"Why not?" I asked.

Goody Hawkins leaned in close. "She told 'em outright that the ministers had no right to say who is a saint and who is a sinner. Said that we could figure that out for ourselves. Stood right up at meetin' and said so. Pastor Wilson was outraged! I can see his face as clearly now as I did that day—all puffed up and ready to burst. Think on it, dearie. Why do the ministers call themselves saints and the rest of us sinners? Seems to me she had a point."

She winked at me and drew loudly on her pipe. I shifted uneasily on my stool.

"Pretty soon the entire village was takin' sides. Pastor Wilson feared he'd lose his church if he couldn't keep a lid on boilin' tempers. Things got so contentious, the elders feared rebellion. Still, she told 'em, and these were her words: 'You can preach no more than you know.' Thing is, she thought she knew more than everybody else!" Goody Hawkins laughed outright, but I saw not the humor in it.

"What happened? What did the elders do?" I prompted.

"Two of the ministers were on her side—John Cotton and John Wheelwright—peas in a pod they were, and they protected her. But the governor watched and waited to catch her breakin' a law. Figured he'd wait her out. In the meantime, the terrible thing happened."

A slow exhale of smoke obscured her weathered face. When it cleared, she wore an expression that frightened me.

"What terrible thing?" I asked outright.

"The thing that revealed her pact with Mistress Dyer—and the Devil."

"Are you saying that they were witches?" I braced myself for the scandal that Merry had told me of.

"Not so fast, dearie." She leaned her head against the chair-back. "Mistress Dyer and Mistress Hutchinson were great friends, you see. Mind you, when they weren't talkin' the Scriptures and slanderin' the ministers, they'd go about their womanly duties right properly—attendin' to the sick and the needy. I accompanied them on many an occasion with my special healing herbs."

Her expression darkened again and she leaned forward.

"But here's the rub. They looked down on me with their haughty ways. Never thought I was good enough. Them with their fine houses and important husbands, their book learnin'." She knocked her pipe against the wall to empty its ashes.

I waited patiently for her to continue as she sat back again with a faraway look.

"One night," she finally said, "October it was, rainy and as black as that pot when I received word from Mistress Hutchinson that I was to meet her at the Dyer home. I was to bring my remedies—that's all I was told. Nothing more. Mistress Anne met me at the door. Her pallid face told me how anxious and worried she was. Without a word, she took me to Mary who was abed with fearsome pains. With child she was, but her time was yet weeks away. Oh, she was terrible ill, wailing and thrashing. Mistress Anne's remedies had given her no comfort. I did what I could with my special concoctions. We tarried with her long into the night until she had not an ounce of fight left in her. Finally, before dawn, she was delivered."

The old woman paused and looked upward, following the smoke that rose through the hole toward the sky. Her cloudy, lifeless eye never blinked, and I wanted to turn away, but could not, for her words held me fast. "And then we saw it, " she rasped. "It was not a child at all that she gave forth. It was something hideous. A face without a head— two mouths it had and claws for feet. It was a monster—a child of Satan—and it was dead."

I put my hand to my mouth.

"Master William Dyer hid his face and wept at the sight of it. Mistress Anne said nothing at all. Efficient she was, wrapping up the tiny creature, all business like, but I could tell she was keenly distressed. Could scarcely look at the thing. But I wanted a closer examination. And I got it. I can see it clear to this very day."

A half smile crossed Goody Hawkins' face, as though savoring the memory. I shuddered, hugging my knees to my chin. Was she telling the truth? Or was *she* the witch? Who else would tell such a fiendish tale?

She continued. "Minister Cotton was called, and in secret, we dug a hole in the burying ground that night— the three of us—John Cotton, Anne Hutchinson, and I. We broke the law, ye know. A midwife cannot bury a newborn in secret even with a clergyman at her side. If the elders were to find out, well, it would bode great trouble for the Dyers and the Hutchinsons. I cared little for magistrates and ministers and their laws, so I went along with it and kept my mouth shut. The sooner the thing was put in the ground, I said, the better off we all would be."

"Was the secret kept?"

"Sin has its way of making itself known. It was revealed, but not right away."

"How then? When?"

She squinted her good eye, as though deciding whether or not to tell me more. Or perhaps she thought I was about to faint, for by then I was feeling light-headed. She poured more of the black stuff from the pot and continued.

"Even Satan's work would not quiet Anne Hutchinson. The Devil's other harlot, she was, if you want my opinion. The creature was barely cold in its grave when she set to doin' the Devil's next bidding. Got Minister Wheelwright to take over the Boston Church while Pastor Wilson was away to England. This is what she wanted all along—a hand-picked minister to be her mouthpiece. A lovely plan she thought it was, I'm sure…until the old governor got wind of it. He saw his chance to use the law against her. He called Mistress Hutchinson and many others up for judgment."

"On what charges?"

"Sedition—for plotting against Pastor Wilson. I'll never forget that day of the inquisition. Snow lay a yard deep. Bitter cold. It was to take place at the meetinghouse across the river at Newtowne. John Winthrop thought the long journey would keep her followers away. But he was wrong. They came in great numbers, including Mary Dyer. Barely recovered from her illness, she walked all the way to the Charlestown ferry, then five miles along the Indian path, just to be there. I know because I walked it, too, though the skies were dark and filled with snowflakes as great as shillings.

"Governor Winthrop, wanting to make short business of the whole affair, acted both prosecutor and judge. Before the mornin's end, he pronounced Minister Wheelwright guilty and banished him from the colony. He disenfranchised many others for signing a petition on Wheelwright's behalf. One of 'em was William Dyer, Mary's husband. Hard thing for a man like him to lose his standin' in the colony. Had to surrender his arms that day. Imagine a man to be without arms in the wilderness."

"And Mistress Hutchinson?"

"She was summoned in the afternoon. Mind you, not a person had left the meetinghouse. Not for cold nor hunger was a single man or woman goin' to miss this interrogation.

"Tall and straight into the meetinghouse she walked, like she were Queen Bess, herself. The first person she saw was Mary Dyer. I was watching 'em. Their eyes met. Only Satan knows what kind of pact they had between 'em."

I shifted uncomfortably again, knowing I ought not to be listening to talk of black magic!

"The governor and magistrates questioned Mistress Hutchinson all afternoon long. Oh, you should have heard it, dearie. She outwitted 'em on every point. She outwitted 'em with words straight from Scripture.

"She was judged innocent, then?" I asked hopefully.

"Don't hurry me, child! The governor called for a *second* day of questioning, and that's when he got her. That's when the cat got his mouse." She clapped her hands together like the jaws of an animal trap.

"Got her? What did she say?"

"Claimed the Lord spoke directly through her."

I sat upright in my chair in surprise.

"Imagine a mere woman proclaiming herself the mouthpiece of the Lord! In the time it takes a pauper to ride a good horse to hell, he declared her views blasphemous and banished her outright!"

"Banished her? From the colony? Forever?"

"Not before extending her 'mercy,'" answered Goody Hawkins with a devious smile. "The winter was so severe for travel that he let her stay—until the month of March—under house arrest at the home of Thomas Weld over yonder in Roxbury Village."

"Under house arrest? She was not allowed to return to her family?"

"Nor see a single soul that long, cold season. But one person came, nonetheless," she said meaningfully.

"Mary Dyer?" I asked.

"Aye. She walked the icy, windswept fields just to talk with her through the crack of a window. Mistress Dyer told me of it, herself. There was not many she could tell this to, but since I did not reckon with the magistrates, and since we already had one secret between us, I suppose she thought this one safe with me."

Goody Hawkins paused again to refill her pipe. I looked at the squaw, noticing for the first time just how young she appeared to be. Not much older than myself. Her clothes were ragged like Goody Hawkins' and her feet were bare. The infant had awakened; its tiny fist punched the air and it let out a short, strong cry. She shifted it to her other breast. I looked away and returned my attention to the storyteller.

"When spring arrived, Mistress Hutchinson was allowed back into Boston—and that's when she worked her real magic! Seems the magistrates had no *legal* right to banish her because she had never signed the Wheelwright petition. She was a woman. She couldn't sign the Wheelwright petition!" With that, Goody Hawkins doubled over with laughter, which turned into a fit of coughing.

"She tripped 'em up in their own laws. The fools," she said when she had regained her voice.

I had never heard anyone speak so disrespectfully about the elders before and I was feeling most distressed. If anyone else were to witness such blasphemy...I shuddered to think of what might happen. I sorely hoped the story would end soon. "After that, they let her go?" I asked anxiously.

"Not before the *ministers* had their say with her. They wanted Mistress Hutchinson to account for herself in a *church* way. And they had good reason. During her confinement she had been questioned several times about her interpretations. Twenty-nine errors about Scripture they collected against her.

"They carted her back to the meetinghouse. Like the court proceeding in Newtowne all over again, it was. Mary

Dyer was seated directly behind her. The meetinghouse
was full. She was made to stand for hours answerin'
questions. Several times I thought she would faint. Big with
child she was by then, yet they would not let her sit until
the end.

"Things did not bode well for her this time. 'An
instrument of the Devil,' Pastor Wilson called her. 'You had
rather been a husband than a wife,' said Minister Peters.
'You are a liar,'" said John Cotton.

"John Cotton? I thought Minister Cotton was her
friend?"

"Friend," said Goody Hawkins with a dismissive wave
of her hand. "A selfish, timid turncoat, he was, as
changeable as the weather. He'd do anything to save his
own skin, if you ask me."

"Did no one support her then? Did no one stand for
her?"

"Only a few. When a vote was taken, they
excommunicated her. 'I do cast you out,' shouted Pastor
Wilson. 'I do deliver you up to Satan,' were his words.
Revenge was his! Finally, John Wilson had brought low
the woman who had slighted him in his own church."

"Poor Mistress Hutchinson," I sighed.

"Poor, indeed!" huffed Goody Hawkins. "She walked
straight past the crowd and held her head high. Only one
person rose to walk with her."

"Mary Dyer?"

"Hand in hand out of the meetinghouse they went as
haughty and defiant as can be! It gave me a strange feelin'
seein' 'em so, knowin' what I knew about 'em."

I thought of Mary Dyer hand in hand with William
Robinson and Marmaduke Stevenson.

"Then someone hollered from the crowd," continued
Goody Hawkins. "'Who is that woman, with Anne
Hutchinson?' Well, John Cotton himself supplied the
answer. 'She is the mother of a monster!'" he cried.

"There can be no more commotion at the gates of Hell than there was at the door of Boston Church that day. They made John Cotton give full account of our secret. Then they got to me. I was ordered to testify or else be jailed...or worse."

"What did you tell them," I asked with astonishment.

"I told 'em all about the monster child. What else was I supposed to do, dearie! For my troubles, they called me a witch and said they would look for other charges against me."

She spat into the fire. The blackened spittle jumped and crackled in the heat. Then, she leaned back again and closed her eyes. I knew not if she were sleeping or in a trance for the time she took. All the while I grew increasingly troubled. Finally, she said, "Worst of all, they barred me from attendin' women in their time of need. Forbid me to meddle in surgery or physicks or oils."

"And so I removed myself to this little cottage. They would just as soon hang me for a witch for what I know about the roots of the forest as for anything else." She tucked her hands underneath her shawl and aimed her good eye at me. "They can call me what they like, but I know who really consorts with Satan. And the truth of it has been revealed!"

The truth. Could Goody Hawkins really speak the truth? I knew not what to make of her tale, but there remained one more question, which I needed to ask.

"And my mother. What do you know of my mother in this?"

She leaned forward and grasped my wrist with her bony hand. Breath heavy with tobacco, she whispered, "She was there. I never told, but she was there!"

"Where?" I asked with alarm.

"At the birth of the monster. Just as we were taking the creature to Minister Cotton, she arrived, remaining behind to tend to Mistress Dyer. But she beheld it with her own eyes. I saw her look."

I recoiled from her ugly face. Now, I knew she must be lying. My mother would never have taken part in such wickedness. "If she were there," I demanded to know, "why did you not tell?"

"To save her from trouble. Your father had forbid her to come to Mary Dyer on account of her friendship with Mistress Anne. But she came anyway. She disobeyed him."

"Liar!" I wanted to yell.

"But I told not a single soul. I kept her secret," she said.

"Why?" I asked.

"She was not like them other two. She didn't have the fire in her eyes. Oh, she may have attended the meetin's and hung on their every word, but she never disturbed nobody. She held her tongue, she did, at least in public."

Why did she sound so convincing? Why did I almost believe her?

"When the other two finally left for Portsmouth Colony with their husbands and families, your mother became quiet in her ways. I hardly saw her after that. Except on her deathbed—on the night your father called on me desperate for help."

"On the night I was born, you mean?"

"Aye. So desperate that he risked trouble with the elders by havin' me attend her."

Father going behind the elders' backs! For mother's sake!

Goody Hawkins sighed. "But it was too late."

Yes, it was too late, I thought. Father had acted too late.

Goody Hawkins' voice turned gentle, "That's how I know you. I've always known you. And that's why I've told you this story. I saw it when you were a mere infant in my arms, that you were meant to know the truth."

Truth. That word again. All it did was confound me. How was the truth to be found among so much disagreement, so many secrets?

There was a long silence. And then I asked what had become of Mistress Hutchinson after she had been banished from the colony.

"Oh, dearie, don't you know what everyone else on God's earth knows?"

I shook my head.

"Killed by Indians in a raid along with all of her children but one. God's punishment, to be sure."

I imagined the scene, the horror of it. Children running. Cries for mercy. Blood. Were they small ones, the children? I did not want to know. "God's punishment." His wrath must have been great. And then something became clear to me. God had punished Mother just as he had punished Anne Hutchinson. They had not been proper goodwives. It was for this that Father would not honor her. It was for this that he could not bear the mention of Mary Dyer's name. And it was for this that he would send me away to England.

My head was beginning to ache. It was time to go. I tried to collect myself and put on a good face so as to be polite, for even a beggar woman like Goody Hawkins deserved kindness, especially when she had offered me drink, which seemed a luxury in this poor place. I will watch for you at market. I will give you bread I told her. But really, I was not certain I wanted to see her again. As I said good-bye, I turned to the Indian squaw, who looked at me with steady, black eyes and what I thought was the glimmer of a smile.

Chapter Eight

Sunday Meeting

Sunday meeting gave me no relief from my misery. My mother was a sinner and no redemption on my part could change this awful fate. At the ringing of the bell I went as usual with Merry and her mother to the Winslow's pew. Surrounded as I was by friends and neighbors who I had known all my life, Patience Burrows, Nellie Colburn, Constance Brown, and their children, I felt as though I did not belong. What was wrong with me? Had the Devil got hold of me with his claws? I had deceived Father. I had let myself be swayed by the sinful Quaker woman. I had listened to blasphemy from the mouth of Goody Hawkins. I prayed, therefore, for deliverance—prayed that God would smite Satan with a blow so hard that I would be set free to become a good daughter once again.

Then, Merry pinched me in the leg and I came to my senses. Stifling a giggle, she elbowed me and cocked her head in the direction of the men's side of the congregation. On more than one occasion Merry had earned a scolding from Pastor Wilson for smiling in church. Even the tithingman was on to her. Although more likely to knock the head of a fidgety boy with his stick, the tithingman would have cracked her good by now, I truly believed, if it were not for Captain Winslow's position. Merry, oblivious to anyone's faultfinding of her, would not sit still until I looked across the aisle. This I did as inconspicuously as possible. Old Man Isherwood's head was thrown back in an open-mouth snore. This did not amuse me and I let Merry know by the scowl on my face.

"No, over there," she whispered. "He's trying to get your attention!"

This time I turned. That is when I saw him. Will Stoddard. He was looking at me and smiling. I faced forward again. The heat on my face should have been enough to keep my eyes from wandering and my neck from craning, but I had not the power, and I stole a second glance just to be sure of what I had seen. Will, feeling the eyes of the tithingman upon him, stopped smiling. Merry put her hand to her mouth to stifle another giggle as her mother gave her a stern look. To avoid a scolding from Mistress Winslow, which I would take far more seriously than her own daughter, I shut my eyes to pray. At the same time, a hush came over the congregation. All coughing and shuffling of feet ceased as if on cue as Pastor and Mistress Wilson entered, followed by Ministers Norton and North, Governor Endicott, Richard Bellingham, and several clergymen and magistrates. This was not the time to trifle and I repented of it, pushing Satan, the state of my craven soul, and Will Stoddard from my mind. My full attention would be Pastor Wilson's, so that I would listen and learn.

After escorting Mistress Wilson to the front pew, the pastor mounted the pulpit. He adjusted his spectacles, looked down upon us to study the day's attendance, and produced an hourglass from the pocket of his longcoat, which he set squarely in front for the benefit of all to see. I watched the tiny grains of sand trickle through as he cleared his throat noisily. He began with a solemn prayer and spoke to its meaning for about a quarter of an hour. Then, teacher Norton spoke to the second commandment; then Pastor Wilson began the sermon. By then, it was nearly time to turn the hourglass again.

"In all ages," he said resoundingly, "God has risen up excellent persons to provide us with patterns to imitate. In our own age, He has given us worthy leaders—men such as our first governor, John Winthrop who, like Moses, led us to a New Jerusalem in the wilderness, so that we might see God's ways and plant a garden."

He smiled through small eyes. I was much encouraged. My sore heart sought his benevolence. I so longed to think that his recent fury on Boston Common was but an aberration, that I would not be infected by Goody Hawkins' version of his treatment of Anne Hutchinson. I wanted the wisdom of his words to convert all of us wrongdoers, so that there would be no further cause for angry judgment and harsh punishment.

"Indeed, John Winthrop's worthy successor, Governor Endicott, has shown us the way to righteousness through his wise governance," he continued. Governor Endicott nodded and puckered his mouth grimly.

"Yet, there are false prophets among us—impostors who must not be imitated." Pastor Wilson paused and I stiffened. "False prophets." I sensed the thunder coming with those ominous words, and come it did with a force that nearly jolted me from my seat.

"Rather, like a weed or a stone," he bellowed, jabbing a finger violently into the air, "we must cast them out so that our garden can grow!"

I dared not move for fear he might be referring to me.

Then, he lowered his voice and in a mocking tone said, "They boast of an 'inner light.' They say they 'listen to the silence' so as to communicate directly with God. This is blasphemy! This is the unleashing of passion! When man acts more from heart than head, should not his madness be restrained with chains, when it cannot be restrained otherwise?"

The congregation rumbled in agreement. I shifted my eyes from side to side. Pastor Wilson held everyone in his thrall. Even Merry looked all flushed and stirred, whereas most sermons left her bored and indifferent.

"The doctrines of the cursed sect of Quakers must not be spread amongst our people, lest we be forever lost in the wilderness, no better than the barbarians who roam this land, like unrepentant children of Eve."

I thought of the squaw and her infant, roaming, unrepentant, and hoped that the pastor would not look directly at me, for it is well known that a saint knows a sinner when her thoughts are unpure. I watched him carefully, then, for a sign. He grasped the sides of his lectern, leaned forward, and passed an accusing eye over all of us. Only when he began searching the bench behind me did I breathe a little easier. But Pastor Wilson was not through. Patches of red appeared on his face and his voice trembled. It was that same expression again. The same expression he wore on Boston Common. "Our laws are the will of the Lord. Impostors to our age and blasphemers of the holy book must...be...put...to...death."

The last words echoed off the walls, chilling me to the bone. I looked across the aisle at Father. His arms were folded tightly, his face dark and inscrutable. I felt miles apart from him. Pastor Wilson continued in this vein for the remainder of the second hour and a full hour more. The words did not have the intent I had desired. Rather, they clang and rioted inside my head, and as sinful as this be, I found myself trying to block them out in order to listen to the silence, like a Quaker. But sin I did not, for in the end I could not hear the stirrings of my soul through all the roar.

When the sermon was over, we ceased for nooning at the Sabbath House before the start of the afternoon service. The mood was somber. The men gathered at one end of the room to discuss the rightness of the pastor's sermon, while Merry and I and some of the other girls helped the women serve biscuits and cider. I went about this task quickly, for I had, after much pondering about Merry's ability to keep a secret, decided to tell her about my visit with Jane Hawkins. I would have to do so without delay, for there was little time and much to tell, especially when I expected Merry to be full of words about Will Stoddard. Quakers and sin, despite her earlier flush, would not be her gravest concern. As for myself, I thought I had successfully put Will out of my mind, yet I noticed him when he came into the room, and my hand trembled when I offered him a cup. I had convinced myself that the smile had been more for Merry's benefit than mine, but now I was not as certain.

After everyone had been served, Merry and I took our refreshments to a bench in the far corner of the room. I was about to tell her Goody Hawkins' tale when Hetty Shepherd joined us. Hetty was a kind and pious girl whose father was a clergyman. I greatly enjoyed her company between services on Sunday, finding it a welcome relief to Merry's sometimes tiresome chatter. But today was different. Hetty's reserve was great and her acts of charity renown—she and her mother distributed food baskets to the poor even though they lived a meager life themselves. So good was she, that I was too ashamed to reveal my story. Perhaps I would have the chance to tell Merry at the spring where we could speak more freely. For now, I decided to keep it to myself. It was just as well, for Merry was full of Will Stoddard, indeed.

"Go on," she said, elbowing my side. "Go and speak with him."

"No," I said, hushing her. Merry may invite flirtations, but I was not as forward as all that. And being under the ever watchful eyes of Patience Burrows, Nellie Colburn, and Constance Brown, I did not want to call attention to myself. They would be sure to tease or scold or warn, and it would all be for naught, for Will was nothing to me. Just a boy who smiled and blushed as boys will do. And then there was Father. To risk his further disapproval was unthinkable.

This much I knew about Will. He was an orphan with few connections. His parents along with his siblings had died from an outbreak of fever on their crossing from England. He was bonded to Thomas Keane and his wife, keepers of the tavern. I often saw Will at market, carrying sacks of flour to the tavern kitchen or tending horses in the stable. The tallness of him and hair the color of cinnamon were difficult to miss, and he was always ready with a friendly wave. He had an honest, open face and seemed to know everyone in town. Once, at John and Martha Ballantine's houseraising, he entertained all with a balancing act along the ridgepole of the roof, making a show of himself and playing jester to the crowd. Everyone laughed and cheered except Father who called him a fool for confusing work with play. I knew not whether Will had ambitions, but in Father's mind, he was merely a servant. Only of late had he started attending Boston Church. There was something else about Will. He was already seventeen and friendly with lots of girls—girls much fairer than I. Merry, for instance, or even Hetty with her delicate chin and stately carriage were much more apt to turn a head.

Here I was contemplating the assumed flattery of a boy on a Sunday; I felt ashamed. That is when I had resolved again to think of my duty and improving the state of my wretched soul. Then, Will Stoddard sat down across from us. Merry nudged me again and I felt my face go red. He nodded hello which caused Merry to sit up smartly. She opened her mouth to begin some kind of prattle with him when Daniel Putnam sat down and got Will's attention instead with the subject of horses. In the meantime, Goody Burrows signaled Merry, Hetty and me for the tidying.

"She mistakes us for servants," Merry said from the corner of her mouth.

"Come," answered Hetty, taking the reluctant Merry by the hand. "Be glad. It's the Lord's day and we have food enough left over for baskets for the poor." Merry rolled her eyes at me as she let Hetty lead her away. Truly, I feared for Merry's boldness and was about to tell Hetty that I would go with her to distribute the baskets, when I was prevented from doing so by Will, rising in mid-sentence with Daniel, to stand in my way.

"Come walk with me on Saturday next," he said, "when I shall have the afternoon free."

I could feel the eyes of Merry and Hetty upon me from across the room. I hesitated. "No," I stammered, "it is not possible. I am sorry."

"Sunday then, after meeting I will walk you home."

"No, I am sorry," I repeated, hurrying away.

I felt at once relieved and miserable. It was an utterly new and disquieting feeling. I quickly rejoined my friends.

"What did he say?" asked Merry excitedly. Even Hetty was wide-eyed with curiosity.

"He asked me to walk with him."

"And?"

"I said no."

"You simpleton! You prefer to go around all glum-faced, miles from town with no one but your Father and stupid goats and chickens to talk to!"

"Merry, really, not here," I said. "Come, we must go."

The congregation began filing out to resume the afternoon service. I quickly turned my back to keep Merry from further talk on the matter. The air revived me as I stepped outside, face against the wind, and strode purposely along the path toward the meetinghouse. I looked forward to Psalms and prayers and hymns. I wanted my mind occupied with spiritual matters and not with worldly distractions that only caused a person grief.

Chapter Nine

The Tavern

Signs of winter were all about. A light, freezing rain crackled against the earth, hardened now by the season's frost. My breath made fleeting clouds in the cold air. In naked branches I saw fingers clutching heavenward for sustenance. In grey clouds I saw faces of desolation. It was December, bringing with it black nights and days so bright with snow your eyes hurt and your ears hum to the utter stillness of it all. It was always in December that I wished Father and I lived in town, for winter can seem unending out at Plouder's Point when the farms are at rest and the roads impassable.

A gust of wind blew down from the Trimount hills, hurrying me from one lane into the next and practically depositing me right at the foot of my destination, Keane's Tavern. I leaned heavily to push open the door. Heat from the massive hearth greeted me, followed by a blend of smells—bread baking, stew on the fire, pipe tobacco, and beer.

It was not often that I went into the tavern, and never without Father, but this time necessity required I go alone. That morning, Father had taken to bed with a terrible chill. It caused me great alarm because Father was seldom ill. I offered to fetch Doctor Quince, but Father protested, saying purgings and bleedings were not for him. I even pleaded for permission to go for Goody Burrows' healing herbs, but he wanted nothing of her "vile physicks." What he needed, he said, was rum. With none in store, I offered to go to Keane's Tavern. At first he protested, saying the way was too far, the cost too dear, and that he'd soon be on the mend in any case. That is when I thought of the ledger. When I pointed out that Master Keane still owed ten shillings for a board and bench, he said he would consider it. In the meantime, I layered every quilt we possessed upon him, yet he still shivered and complained of aching something fierce from limb to limb. "I am going, Father," I had simply said, taking my cloak from the peg. I feared what might happen if he were not tended to soon. Since he was too weak to object, I left immediately, even though the prospect of seeing Will Stoddard caused me some trepidation. I intended to complete my errand quickly and avoid him altogether.

It being mid-day, there were several patrons about, two old men sitting hunched over pewter mugs in the far corner of the room, a small group of soldiers, and a man and woman who wore the weary look of travelers. Mistress Keane emerged from the kitchen with steaming bowls for her customers. A fleshy woman with hair the color of a squirrel and quick, precise movements to match, Dorothy Keane was not one for small talk, usually showing a bit of impatience, what with cooking and keeping rooms and greeting grumpy wayfarers at all hours of the night. She seemed surprised to see me and in a hurry to get back to her kitchen, so I got right to the point about the rum, and handled the matter of the debt to Father as delicately as I knew how.

Mistress Keane was happy to oblige and produced a jar from the kitchen straight away. "What your father also needs is a good, strong poultice and some rabbit stew. I'd send a pot with ye, Hannah, but I've only enough for dinnertime." I began to thank her for her kindness and to tell her that troubling her for the rum was quite enough when she began calling out Will's name.

"Where *is* that boy?" she said. "I told him to get me more rabbits today. If you can wait or come back, we'll clean one for ye, Hannah, to take home with ye."

I started in again with thanks, backing towards the door so I could make my leave, when Will came bounding up from the cellar with a barrel to his shoulder.

"There ye are, Will. Hannah here needs some meat to take home. Hannah, why don't you go along with Will? Keep him company. I'll send Thomas to deliver the rum to your father and to look in on him and tell him you'll be delayed. He's heading out your way right soon with the wagon to pick up some fish at Plouder's Point."

Will dropped the barrel to the floor and smiled.

I explained that Father needed me and that I should return forthwith, but Mistress Keane, perhaps because she was so used to running the tavern, had a way of telling people what to do without ever acknowledging a contrary answer. Whether she knew of Will's interest and was acting as his fellow conspirator or was simply trying to be helpful to me, I knew not. But I found myself consenting to go with him, telling myself it was for Father's own good, albeit against my better judgment.

And that is how I came to walk with Will Stoddard, after all, on a frosty afternoon.

I had never been alone with a boy before, at least not since I was a child with a playmate. Unsure of what to do with my hands, my eyes, anything, I found to my surprise that being with Will was not as difficult as I had imagined. As we walked along by way of Muddy River, he told stories—stories about tavern customers that made me blush and laugh at the same time—sailors who played cards for money and the disreputable women who whispered in their ears. He described how he could always tell the newcomers from England by the dumbstruck looks on their faces when they found how little this town resembled London or Portsmouth or the Boston they knew on the other side. He spoke freely and easily. All I needed to do was listen.

He even told me about his family. About what happened during the crossing on a ship called the *Raven*. Never would I have inquired about such a terrible thing. But he seemed to want to tell. This I found odd, coming from a boy; odd yet somehow right coming from him. And I wanted to know. I wanted to know what it was like to lose everything you loved only to have to begin again, to have your faith and your strength tested to the utmost. In a sense, Father had had to do the same after mother died. I thought, too, of the day when I might be tested—when I might need to make a similar crossing and a similar beginning—in England with my aunt.

Will said the fever had struck terrible and swift. One by one his three siblings died, starting with the youngest, a boy of six named Ethan, then the girls Sarah and Martha, ages nine and ten. His mother took what linens she had brought with her and used them as winding sheets to wrap their bodies for as proper a burial as one could have at sea. Just days later, his father died. All the while, his mother continued to tend to the many others who were sick on board, going without sleep and with barely enough food, giving Will her share of what little there was to go around. Finally, her strength gave out, too, and she took to bed. When she died, Will said he thought he would go mad, what with dismal cries of the grieving, the stench of cattle in the hold, and the pall of death all about. He knew not why Providence had saved him, and as sinful as it was, he thought many times of throwing himself to the sharks and the bottomless sea. The only thing that kept him from doing so, he said, was a promise made to his mother in her final hour that he would live for all of them, that he would carry on the family name once he was safely delivered to these shores.

Thirty people died in all during those ten weeks at sea. The survivors called themselves the fortunate ones, but it was some time before Will could count himself among them, so black was his spirit. The Keanes had taken him in as a bond-servant and they had been kind. Yet, he told me how a day never passes without thoughts of his family, how creaking ropes and howling wind still ring in his ears, how he dreams of winding sheets in frigid, churning waters.

And then he apologized for going on about such sadness, but I did not mind and I told him so. He smiled and his mood brightened. All of that was behind him now, he said. He would work hard and look to his future. He had a plan. As soon as he had paid the debt of his family's passage, he would become an apprentice to a trade. When he had saved enough money, he would buy land and work a farm. In time, he would take a wife.

I had listened to his story with pity, admiring his courage. But the more he spoke about his future, the more I looked to myself. He was certain and confident of what he would do with the years that lay ahead of him. But what plans did I have? Rather, what plans were being laid *for* me? What did I hope for? I did not know. I felt dull and ignorant. I had been nowhere but a few miles outside this town with nothing but an occasional wedding or christening to break the sameness of my days. I wanted to tell him about the recent discoveries that weighed heavily upon me, but trying to find the right words and the right beginning only made me tongue-tied. Neither of us spoke for some time, yet I found no discontent in it. I knew that I wanted to be his friend.

We came to a spot where we decided to watch for rabbits. Will filled his musket with powder while I sat upon a large rock and watched the river flow. A flock of geese squawked overhead. I looked up to realize that the wet cold had gone and that the sun now peeked intermittently from behind fast-moving clouds. I followed the geese with my eyes. What a beautiful sight they made, winging along in perfect formation against the sky. It made me wonder— how was it that God's lesser creatures could find harmony when his people could not?

It was almost as though Will had read my thoughts. "Did you hear what happened at the meetinghouse yesterday?" he asked.

I shook my head no.

"Governor Endicott wrote a letter to Parliament to justify the hangings. He read it to the people. He boasts of his goodness in sparing Mary Dyer's life."

"Why must he justify his actions to Parliament?" I asked.

"Some say the governor is not as sure of his laws as he pretends."

"What do you mean?"

"The Quakers have important friends in England. Friends who could put the colony's charter at risk if they think our laws have gone too far."

Surely this was the breakthrough I had been hoping for. "If things have gone too far then our laws will be changed!" I cried.

Will laughed. "Not according to the governor," he said. "It's more arrests and beatings for Quakers and their sympathizers if they don't comply."

"And death," I added.

"One thing I know," said Will, taking aim with his musket, "we would all be better off if the Quakers would keep their ideas to themselves." He pressed the trigger. The shot ruptured the air and the acrid smell of burnt powder filled my nostrils. The rabbit darted and escaped.

I sighed. Will was just like everybody else—believing that more cruelty was the answer. Try as I might I could not see the logic in it.

"I sense that you are troubled, Hannah," he said. "It's a hard thing that people die, but John Endicott is a prudent man and we must trust in his wisdom. We must stick together—"

"It is not just the governor and our laws, Will," I interrupted. And then I did a silly thing; I began to cry. I turned my head away. He came and sat by my side. I had been wanting to tell someone about Goody Hawkins' story, about the letter, about Mother's sin and Father's displeasure, but I never thought it would be Will Stoddard. I had no notion of how to begin except to take a deep breath, after which the words gushed like grain through a barrel stave.

"Mary Dyer and my mother were friends many years ago," I said, expecting his disapproval. Will said nothing, letting me continue in my own way. "They were followers of Anne Hutchinson, the woman they banished."

"Yes, I have heard tell of her."

"I fear that God punished my mother for that unholy friendship—by taking her life at the moment she gave me mine." And then I told him everything—from the time I witnessed the hangings to my visit to Jane Hawkins' cottage. I left out none of the details, not even the lurid parts about the monster birth. Will neither flinched nor condemned; he simply listened.

"That was a long time ago," he said when I had finished.

"Now I know why Father never speaks of her. She disobeyed him. He hates her for being a bad wife. That is why he hates Mary Dyer and people like her. That is why he wants to send me away."

"Perhaps it isn't hate, Hannah. Perhaps it is grief."

Will had certainly known grief; I could see it in his eyes. Funny, how at that moment, they made me think of Father's.

"All of the bad business must have made it very hard on a man like your father, and then to lose his wife. But he has made it right again with the elders. There is not a more just man in the county than Jonah Pryor, and I do not believe for a moment that he wants to send you away."

Father, a just man. I had always thought so and wanted to think so still. I wrapped my arms around my legs, resting chin to knees, and listened to the whispering of Muddy River.

"Do you know what I think?" said Will. "I think that God did not intend to punish. Not when He blessed Jonah with you."

I looked into his face. The sunlight made ripples of color in his hair. He stood, extending his hand. I took it. It felt warm and strong. I rose and brushed the twigs from the back of my skirt.

"I know you're wanting to get back to your father. Let me take you by way of a place where I *know* I can find a rabbit or two."

Managing a smile, I agreed to go on, for there was joy to be had even on this cold day, and I would praise the Lord for it with gladness and thanks.

Chapter Ten

Preacher in the Wilderness

We walked away from the river and into a meadow at the edge of the wood. There beside a quiet stream were the remains of a Pequot village; its inhabitants gone now to the ravages of the smallpox and to John Endicott's purge of many years ago. Will often hunted there, he said, making use of the small rock fireplaces and the shelters of bearskins still draped on frames of birch. He liked this place and said he wanted to show it to me, that he would have a rabbit or two in no time, and I would soon be on my way home to Father.

As promised, and with two clean shots of his musket, Will had his rabbits. He placed the poor creatures in a sack from his pocket and suggested we take a shortcut through the wood to hasten our way home. With Will at my side, I entered it with nary a thought of witches or spirits lurking along my path. It was a pretty walk, even at this time of year, and one I had never taken before.

We were not long into our passage, however, when we heard the unexpected sound of a voice. Whether it belonged to an Indian, a hunter, or a robber we knew not, but instinct told us to proceed cautiously. My heart beat a little faster as we stopped to determine from which direction it was coming. Listening carefully, we decided that it was a woman's voice—an English woman's voice, a discovery which may have made us less wary but no less curious. It was coming from our right, beyond a small incline where two massive rocks blocked a clear view. We approached to peer around the granite wall. There in the middle of a tiny clearing stood a woman dressed in a long grey cloak. Surrounding her in a half-circle were about a dozen people, some seated on the ground, some on fallen pine limbs— men, women, and a few young children. A pile of twigs burned for warmth. I quickly scanned the group for a familiar face, and recognized Black Joseph, servant to Edward Hull, one of the wealthiest men in the colony. Joseph always had a nod and a smile for me at market. Even more surprising than Joseph's presence, however, was the sight of two Indian males and the squaw I had seen at Goody Hawkins' cottage, her baby snug in an animal skin tied to her back. They sat cross-legged and slightly apart from the rest of the crowd. English men and women, Indians, and a black man all together listening to a woman speak— my eyes must have blinked several times to make sure I was not dreaming. In the instant she turned her head, I recognized the woman to be none other than Mary Dyer.

Will and I looked at one another. He took my elbow and started to move away. "You *do* know who that is, don't you?" he whispered. "We do not belong here!"

"Hush," I said, straining to listen.

"They say our tests of virtue are too simple," said the Quaker woman. "They accuse us of false pride and arrogance. They say we follow our passions and obey and not obey as we see cause. This is unjust. *We* say that every man and woman should walk as their conscience persuades them, every one in the name of the Lord."

I am certain that Will pulled my elbow more than once, but I found myself incapable of moving.

"The Lord has a mission for every one of you," she continued. "You must work to discover your own assignment. Tell me *not* of what you have of material possessions. Tell me *not* of what you do to show that you are good and worthy of salvation. Rather, tell me of the *Holy Spirit* that is *within* you."

I realized then that here, in the middle of the wood by the side of a rock, I was witnessing a sermon. This woman was preaching. Though her congregation be small and her church nothing but the open air, like Pastor Wilson or Reverend Norton, this woman was preaching. Yet her voice was like music and her words were like song. She did not thump and thunder and turn red of face, but neither did her gentleness belie her authority, for she held her listeners with a power that was a marvel to behold.

"Hannah, we must be gone," beseeched Will.

"Let us stay a moment," I insisted.

"They break the law!" he said pointing to the gathering.

I must have been overzealous in my pleading to stay, because just then, Mary Dyer stopped and looked in our direction.

"Away, quickly," said Will, this time with a firm tug of my arm.

"Come," she called out with the same even gentleness, "you are welcome here. We are all Friends."

My entire being stiffened as Will and I exchanged a look of dread, for it had not been my intention nor his to be discovered. But discovered we had been. I took a reluctant Will by the sleeve and without a word we walked toward the clearing. The followers made a place for us on the bare ground close to the fire. I nodded at the Indian squaw who returned the acknowledgment with the same inscrutable gaze as before. Black Joseph smiled at me.

Once we had taken our places, she continued her sermon about the workings of the Holy Spirit. She said that one divines an inner light only when one truly seeks it. She said that it is only in silence that one actually hears its workings within. She encouraged us right then and there to listen to the silence. And we did. For several minutes we listened to nothing but the occasional falling bough and the rustling wind. Now and again, someone would break the silence to share a story. One woman rose to say that it was only a profound stirring of her soul—a moment of revelation that God had a plan for her—that kept her from drowning herself after the deaths of her three small children from the smallpox. I looked at Will for his reaction, sensing that this must have touched him to the core, but I could not judge it, for he kept his eyes fastened to the ground. Mary Dyer looked to the woman with kindness and said: "When we know in our souls of the light within, we can overcome great hardships and trials. Only *you* can feel such power. No one else can tell you of it."

Another woman rose to say, "Some preachers claim that women have no souls."

"No more than a goose, I've heard tell!" returned Mary with a smile. "But as we know from Scripture, the soul knows no difference of sex, nor of station in life, nor of the color of skin."

Then Black Joseph rose. In a strong voice, he described his voyage as a very young man from his home far across the sea. Taken by force from his village and his family, bound in chains, bruised and beaten and sick with fever, with little food or water to sustain him, he found the strength to survive because he felt the Almighty's power. Only later did he call this power his Christian Lord, but he knew all the same that His presence had saved him. A profound silence lingered until Mary Dyer responded to the remarkable tale.

"Every captured creature under the whole Heaven," she said, "deserves liberty and freedom. And that is why we are here. We who seek to end the persecution of the innocent—whether they be enslaved in chains or imprisoned by laws—are servants of the Lord. I have returned to this colony seeking only the truth, knowing it will set us free."

Every captured creature under the whole Heaven deserves liberty and freedom. The soul knows no difference of sex, nor of station in life, nor of the color of skin. Such strange words. Such new ideas. What to make of them, I knew not. This must be the blasphemy the ministers warned against, for I had never heard such a sermon at Sunday meeting. So confused was I that I hardly realized that the service had ended. Everyone was standing and nodding their departure to one another.

"Now, Hannah, away," said Will.

"I must go to her," I answered. I knew I was asking much of Will, who had remained against his better judgment and only for my sake, so I offered that he be on his way immediately without me. He refused.

"I will wait over yonder," he said, leaving me to face the preacher alone. I turned to see the mysterious squaw depart with her companions. Will is right, I thought. We should leave with great haste. Suddenly, I felt afraid of Mary Dyer and the ice blue of her eyes. I took one step backward as she bade farewell to Black Joseph with a firm clasp of both her hands. I stopped, holding tight to the edges of my cloak, thinking, if I stay what will I say to her? What will she say to me? Black Joseph moved off and only I remained now. Seeing me standing fast, she looked at me with those eyes.

"I am not a Quaker," I blurted, just like the ninny that Merry accuses me of being. She looked at me slightly bemused, I thought. I felt foolish at my awkwardness and started again. "I mean to say, I am not a follower, but I am moved by your words."

This time the eyes peered back at me with so much warmth that the ice melted and all fear was washed away. "And I am very happy that you are here," she replied.

"We were not spying, my friend and I. We happened upon your meeting by chance and could not help but stay to listen."

"There are spies enough in these woods," she said without a trace of fear. "I know that it is not for reporting but for seeking that you come. What is your name, child? I feel that you are familiar to me."

"I saw you on that day...on the road to Boston Common."

"I see," she replied, seemingly with more pity for me than for herself.

"I am told, Mistress Dyer, that you knew my mother many years ago, Elizabeth,...wife of Jonah Pryor. I am her daughter, Hannah." She studied my face for so long that I was convinced she did not remember. Perhaps Goody Hawkins had told falsehoods, I thought, feeling that I would perish on the spot if Mistress Dyer could tell me nothing.

Those few moments seemed like an eternity until she brushed my cheek lightly and said, "Yes, of course. You are so like her."

Just then, one of two men standing by with horses readied for departure, called out, "It is not safe to tarry long, Mistress."

These words caused me considerable dismay, I must confess, and I searched the edges of the clearing with my eyes for signs of guards or spies sent by the governor to report on the Quakers. Except for Will looking miserable, no one was in sight.

"A few moments, please," she answered, taking me by the hand and guiding me to sit beside her on a trunk of pine. "Your mother was a dear friend to me. She provided comfort in an hour of great need. I know that she was taken from you at your birth. That was a great sorrow to me as it was to all who knew her."

"Mistress Dyer, I wonder if you can help me?"

"Yes, child, if it is within my power."

"There is something I wish to know about her but the knowledge is hard to come by."

"Go on."

"I wish to know...was she...was she a godly woman?"

"Why child, she was a godly woman, indeed."

"That is not what Father thinks." I looked down to hide my shame. "He thinks her death God's punishment for wrongdoing."

"God does not seek vengeance. It was her time to go to Him."

"No! I do not believe it!" I said. "She died because of you! The Devil's harlot!"

There, I had said it. I had said words that were poisoning my thoughts. Tears spilled from my eyes, but at that moment, I was not sorry; I was glad. "Why did you not leave her alone," I said. "Leave her alone to be a goodwife."

Had she turned her back on me and departed forthwith, I would not have blamed her. Instead she placed an arm around my shoulder and said, "Child, it is very difficult, but there are things you will understand in time."

I wiped my eyes. "I wish to understand now," I answered.

"All right. I will try to explain." Mistress Dyer put her hands together in thought. "Your mother and I had known one another as girls and our families were well acquainted. Good friends we were with much in common." She smiled and suddenly she seemed younger and gayer in spirit. "So delighted was I when she and your father arrived here. She brought a freshness and vitality—and news from home that I so longed to hear! We would talk for hours of the people we had known in London—about books we had read and plays we had seen—pleasant memories—to help us through our difficulties. As you well know, Hannah, this is an unforgiving land, and there was much to learn in order to simply survive. And so we helped each other."

"Was it very hard for her here in the wilderness?"

"At first her heart rose sorely at life in the New World and its new manners, but after she was convinced it was the way of God, she submitted to it. We all did, man and woman alike."

"Was she a goodwife?" I asked.

"She was a devoted goodwife to your father and a most capable midwife, too. So fragile when she arrived and so strong and clever by the time my family and I left for Portsmouth Colony. Not once did she disown our friendship even when there was danger in it."

"What danger? What had you done? I have heard things. Terrible things."

She smiled. "That is for others to say."

"They say you were under a spell. Under the spell of Anne Hutchinson! Is it true? Was she a witch?"

"No, child, she was not a witch," she said gently.

"Then why did she cause such trouble? Why did Father forbid mother to befriend her?"

Taking my hand in her own, she said, "I had a wondrous teacher and devoted friend in Anne Hutchinson. She, however, made our elders extremely unhappy with her ideas. They, in turn, made things difficult for her and for those who listened to her."

"She taught women about the meaning of the Scriptures, did she not?"

"Yes, and your mother was one of her best students. She had a keen and curious mind, your mother, even venturing to disagree with Mistress Hutchinson, herself, on a point from time to time!"

"She was not a *true* follower of Mistress Hutchinson then," I said with some relief.

"Not everyone who attended those meetings held the same opinions, Hannah. Many sought purely to exercise the mind."

"Why did the elders object to the meetings? What was the harm in them?"

"They said that a woman had no right to teach. They said Mistress Anne erred about the Scriptures, that her interpretations were wrongheaded."

"If she knew Scripture exceedingly well, how could this be so?"

"I believe it had more to do with the elders' fear than Anne Hutchinson's error."

It surprised me to hear her criticizing the elders so candidly. She spoke freely like a man, yet seemed not at all aware of this curious condition. Coming from the likes of Goody Hawkins was one thing, but from a gentlewoman, it was quite another.

"It was for her teaching and interpretations that the elders banished her," I stated.

"That and her unrepentant ways," she replied, "and many of us left with her. It was apparent we would fare better *outside* of Massachusetts Bay Colony. Upon leaving, I never saw your dear mother again."

I could not speak for several moments, yet desiring to understand something very important, I mustered a boldness I knew not that I possessed. "Mistress," I said, "they say that you abandoned your children and husband to return to England." I searched her face to see if I had given offense.

"My children and my husband can be no dearer to me than they are and always have been, but I was called by the Lord to do His work," she answered forthrightly.

"And the child, Mistress," I continued, "it pains me to say the words for they are ugly."

"Speak the words, child."

My voice became a whisper. "They say there was a monster child. They say it was Satan's? Is it true?"

This time, she squeezed my hand tightly and looked directly into my eyes. "The Lord sent me that poor, wretched child. To strengthen me so that I would not bend with the burden of His cross."

I took my hand away. "Still, they call you terrible names."

"I tell you with my very being that what they say is untrue."

"They persecute you. Your life is in danger."

"It is not my own life I seek but the life of God's goodness."

"If they were to find you here, preaching, why they'd...," I began, when the dreadful words were cut short by one of the men in her company.

"Mistress!" he shouted. "We must be off while the light is good."

She placed both hands on my shoulders. "I must go. Fret not for your mother's memory. She was the kindest and godliest of women. And fret not for me. A light shines within. The Holy Spirit is my guide."

She rose and embraced me. As she mounted her horse, I was reminded of Judith from the Bible, a devout woman who saved her people from conquest by severing the head of Holofernes, the greatest of their enemies. Fearless with the courage of a warrior is Mary Dyer, I thought. And though words are her weapon, not the sword, she wields them just as mightily.

I looked up into the late afternoon sky. *She was the kindest and godliest of women.* With those words, had I found the truth I had been seeking? I stood there listening to the silence. The sun was giving way to the trace of a full moon, which I knew would help guide Mistress Dyer safely to her destination that night, wherever it might be.

Will came up behind me, and I swung around. He looked frightened and not a little angry. "The woods have eyes and ears, Hannah. Say nothing of this to anyone."

Even Will's apprehension could not disappoint my happiness. "She speaks the truth, Will. She speaks the truth!"

"Yes, I have heard her words," he said gravely.

"Do you not think her virtuous? Do you not think her treatment unjust?" I could scarcely get the words out quickly enough to express how profoundly she had touched me.

"She has the eyes of a mad woman. Don't you see?"

I was stung. "Hush, Will, she is a holy woman!"

"She is an itinerant preacher in the wilderness ranting about an inner light while a noose hangs ready for her at this very moment. Hannah, why do you not see that she is mad?"

Fear, I told myself. It is fear from which he speaks and not from the error of Mistress Dyer's ways, but I said nothing, lest Will begin to think myself mad, too.

Chapter Eleven

Winter

When I returned from Keane's Tavern I found Father sleeping fitfully. His forehead burned with fever and while he was able to acknowledge my presence, he knew not what time of day it was nor how long I had been absent. On a table beside his bed sat the jar of rum and next to it a cup with a spoonful or two inside; Thomas had attended to Father as promised. Still, I was much worried and set about preparing the rabbit stew for supper, but not before I made a poultice of chamomile, crumbs of brown bread and slices of apple mixed with a little water, and a good dose of the rum. I heated the mixture over the fire, wrapped it tight in clean linen, and applied it to Father's chest, wishing that Goody Burrows were present, for I was not at all certain that the concoction was correct. She likely would say that the use of what was handy and getting it good and hot was the thing that made the remedy work, or so I told myself, heating the poultice again and again, even though it meant disturbing Father's rest.

With the good Lord's help, within a few hours, his coughing had eased. Unable to keep from fearing the worst, however, for I have seen illnesses take unexpected and distressing turns, I sat by his bedside 'til the first light of morning. He never did eat a bite of the stew.

Over the following weeks, with the help of merciful Providence, I managed to nurse Father back to health. By then winter was full upon us. Storm after storm sent pounding winds and snow so deep it nearly reached the tops of our windows. For days on end I saw no one and talked to no one but Father, Challenger, the goats, and the chickens. Oh, what Merry would have to say about the sameness of my days! Unlike my less encumbered friend, I busied myself, for it is weary doing nothing. With household chores, the loom, tending the animals, melting ice and snow for water, the hours were full. I also spent a good deal of time in thought. I greatly considered the words of Mary Dyer's sermon and her words to me, of which I had forgotten not a one.

I also thought about Will. One moment I would hear the sound of his voice and feel the touch of his hand. In the next moment I was certain he would never speak to me again. A girl who would willfully break a law was one to be forsaken as quickly as possible. It was clear that Will had stayed only because he dared not leave me alone in the wood. What was he thinking about me now?

Then there was the matter of Father. I had dared not tell him about the encounter with Mary Dyer for fear of the consequences. Neither did he, throughout his illness, share the knowledge of the letter, nor guess my anticipation of it, though I was constantly struck with worry whenever I thought the subject was about to be broached. But it never was. As soon as Father had regained his strength, it seemed to me that he was spending more of his time at work in the shed. Hammering and sawing. Sawing and hammering. The loneliest sounds in the world as the snow continued to fall, day after day.

Aside from writing in my daybook, another great comfort during those long evenings after Scripture reading was to take mother's *Sonnets* to my bed by lamplight. For like the good book's words, they were a balm for my troubles. "Ah but those tears are pearl which thy love sheds, And they are rich, and ransom all ill deeds." I read these words over and over again. It was true, I had shed tears, but would they ransom *my* ill deeds? Had she shed tears? Had mother shed tears in this very book for displeasing Father? I ran my fingers across the pages, yellowed now with age, thinking that perhaps I *am* like her. Was she *really* "the kindest and godliest of women" as I so wanted to believe, or was she a sinner as Father undoubtedly thought? I prayed those nights that some day I would know with certainty. I prayed, too, that I might be pious like Hetty and content like Merry. And always, the last thing I prayed for before I went to sleep was the safety of Mary Dyer.

In mid-winter, the Lord sent us a welcome thaw, and we finally set out to meeting on Sunday after one of the longest absences I can remember. Father also seemed cheered by the rapidly melting snow as we walked along together. Though I knew it was but a brief reprieve, the warmth of the sun on my face and the smell of damp earth in the air made me feel that spring was not so very far away. The sight of folks filling the roads again made it seem as though the entire county had just risen from a long sleep and was stretching its limbs. Life had returned.

Best of all on this day, I would see Hetty and Merry for the first time in weeks—and perhaps Will. My spirits lifted. Knowing my dear friends would be waiting for me outside the meetinghouse made me long to run to them. It took all that I had within to keep myself properlike; but I did quicken my step, noticing, as I did so, that Father matched his pace to mine. For that I was grateful.

When we turned into the meetinghouse yard, the first person I saw was Merry, dressed in what appeared to be a new full-length cape of a very fine wool. She was chatting away, her curls bobbing with more enthusiasm than was befitting for a girl about to attend church. Hetty was listening patiently with her usual serene and slightly bemused expression. I could not help but smile broadly at the sight of them even though it was Sunday.

"We pitied you, Hannah, so far outside of town, and the snow laying perilous deep!" said Merry. "Hetty, of course had her good works to perform. And I was doomed to needlepoint. But you, Hannah, you must have suffered most of all!"

"Mama and I do not suffer for attending the needy," chided Hetty.

"And I had goats and chickens to talk to," I said in jest. "And Father, too!" I added, as he came up behind us, touching his hat to my friends.

"Do not linger, now," he said. "Speak your pleasantries and take your places inside."

"Yes, Father," I said, watching him go and turned to Merry and Hetty.

"Let us meet at the spring tomorrow! I have missed you so. And I have things to tell," I added mysteriously, enjoying the raised eyebrows it caused, especially Merry's. It was walking with Will that I had in mind; about the meeting in the wood, I was not as certain I would confide.

Just then I felt a tap on my shoulder. It was Patience Burrows.

"Tuesday, next, Hannah, I expect to see you," she said. "I've got a quilt on and I'll be needin' another pair of hands. Your hands!"

"Yes, Goody Burrows, I will be there," I replied.

"One good reason to wish for another snowstorm," whispered Merry into my ear.

I shook my head in resignation at her brazenness and steered her into the meetinghouse as her mother beckoned to us to hurry along. We took our usual places. Ever under the watchful eyes of Patience Burrows, Nellie Colburn, and

Constance Brown, I was mindful of not craning my neck
for a glimpse of Will. Nevertheless, I felt the urge of it, yet
kept my eyes lowered, only shifting them slightly for the
sight of him.

Behind me the goodwives had taken to whispering. I
cocked an ear to listen, even while Merry was going on
about a new pianoforte she was begging her father to buy
in England on his next voyage abroad.

"Imagine, flaunting themselves right under the noses
of the magistrates," I heard Patience Burrows say.

"Such boldness is to be feared," said Nellie Colburn.

"Jane Hawkins it was," said Constance Brown,
lowering her voice in her fretful way. "Said the whole lot of
them was gathered in a circle in the wood."

A meeting, I thought. They are talking about a Quaker
meeting!

"Said they was dancin' and carryin' on—men and
women—and children together!"

I could not believe my ears! How could such a thing
be said when I knew that not a bit of it was true! I wanted
to shout out loud that Quaker meetings were not like that
at all!

"Constance Brown!" cautioned Nellie Colburn, "Goody
Hawkins is not to be trusted. You know she's not right in
the head. If anybody has the Devil's ear, it's that one!"

"Well then, have ye heard the news about John
Chamberlain?" said Goody Burrows. "A more upright
Puritan man is not to be found. He denounced the
executions at the prison door and they fell upon him.
Whipped him, they did, and threw him in a cell."

"And Edward Wharton of Salem," whispered Goody
Brown, checking nervously about her. "He spoke out
against the punishments at Thursday meeting last and now
he, too, sits in Boston jail. Makes you wonder what your
own neighbor is up to, don't it?"

"They're tightening the notch, I'd say," said Goody Burrows. "Mark my words. More will find themselves at the foot of the great elm before it's over."

I hardly heard Pastor Wilson's sermon that morning, so sick of heart was I. My thoughts were given to John Chamberlain and Edward Wharton, two more jailed in her name. And what about Goody Hawkins? What had she seen? Was it the meeting that Will and I had attended? Was she there that day, spying in the woods? And where was Will now? Why was he not at the meeting?

The mood at the Sabbath House during the nooning hour was particularly somber. This day had not turned out as happily as it had started. I had hoped to see Will to find that he was not angry with me. I had hoped to tell Merry that I had walked with him and it had been fine. I had hoped that there would be no more whispering about Quakers and punishments and death. None of this had come to pass. None of it. After services had concluded for the day, I felt as though winter had never given pause to hopefulness, for I was filled with foreboding at what Goody Hawkins might have revealed.

That night, I tossed and turned and when sleep came, I dreamed that I was aboard the *Raven*, clinging for my life in a mighty and merciless storm. The dream left me bleary-eyed and out of sorts the next morning. Yet, it did not prevent me from seeing that Father had something important to say.

"Today, the court will hear the cases of those recently arrested for breaking the Quaker laws. I have been called to the jury," he announced during the breakfast meal.

"Yes, Father," I answered.

"The day will be long as several more arrests were made last night."

"Yes, Father?" I said expectantly.

"The menace is spreading," he continued, "and stronger measures had to be taken."

"Who, Father?" I asked. "Who was arrested last night?"

"Will Stoddard, for one!" he replied angrily. "Let that be a lesson to you. That boy is a heathen and his actions prove it. Keep that in mind and see to it that his attentions toward you are discouraged. Don't think I haven't noticed."

"Will! Will Stoddard in Boston Prison!" My heart pounded. "What has he done?" I cried.

"He attended a Quaker meeting with the Dyer woman, herself. The elders had no knowledge that she had re-entered the colony until now."

"Who? Who says this is so?" I shouted. "Will is not a follower!"

"Lower your voice, daughter! Jane Hawkins. Jane Hawkins says it is so."

"The woman people scoff at is taken at her word?" I stood. "I must go to him."

"You will do no such thing!"

"Father, I must."

"You will finish your meal and go on about your chores. That boy and his troubles do not concern you."

I grabbed my cloak off the hook and threw it over my shoulders.

"I forbid you to go, daughter," he said, rising from his chair.

"I am sorry, Father. I am truly sorry," was all I could say as I shut the door firmly behind me.

Chapter Twelve

An Unlikely Friend

I thought my insides would burst with running all the way to Boston Prison. I stopped doubled over at the corner of Prison Lane to catch my breath and decide what to do. When I had calmed myself, I looked around the corner to find about a dozen people assembled at the prison gate. Cold and haggard they looked, as though they had been there half the night. A jailer stood guard with a ready musket, though I daresay, these folk appeared to pose no threat. Farmers, most of them, I would say judging by their dress. I approached quietly. Just then the heavy prison door creaked open and Simon Bradstreet emerged. The group roused themselves from their huddle and a commotion began. They clamored loudly, competing for the magistrate's attention. The jailer took up his weapon, but Master Bradstreet merely brushed them aside and continued on his way without so much as a nod or a word.

I looked into their glum and frozen faces as I worked my way up to the guard. "Pardon, please, pardon," I said, as sympathetically as I could. If only the jailer would get word to Will that I knew of his plight, I thought. Perhaps he will take pity on me and come to my aid. The group looked on with interest.

"Will Stoddard," I said, my voice small and quivering. I tried to speak louder. "Will Stoddard is being held. I would like to see him if I could."

The jailer blinked slowly, dumbly like a cow. "No one can see the prisoners, Missy. Go home where you belong."

"You don't understand. I *must* see him."

"Nobody sees the prisoners, I said."

"Just for a moment...just a word..."

"You're the Pryor girl, aren't ye?"

"Please, I beg you."

"Aye, sure ye are," he said, spreading a smile over broken teeth. "Your father wouldn't be too pleased to see you here, now would he."

I looked away in shame. I should have stayed at home and told Father the truth, I thought. Perhaps he would have agreed to help Will if he knew that I was to blame. Now, I would only anger him further. Oh, it was all my fault. I had never felt so wretched in my life. What was I to do? As I stood there helpless and confused, the prison door opened again. This time it was the marshal. He was leading a young Indian squaw by the elbow—the same Indian squaw I had seen now on two previous occasions—with her infant tied to her back. He was crying loudly. The marshal wore a fierce expression as he pushed the squaw through the crowd.

"Now why is the likes of her getting released while good Christian people languish on the inside," a respectable-looking woman of many years demanded to know.

The marshal ignored the question, roughly deposited the squaw into the lane, and retreated back inside the prison. The squaw, as she passed by, looked at me with those same steady black eyes.

"The squealin' of a little brat sets their teeth on edge when they're dispensin' their legal judgments, don't you know," scoffed the jailer.

"Why had the squaw been arrested?" I dared to ask.

"Savages are not above our laws, you know, Missy. Especially one that shows 'rebellious carriage towards her mistress!' Don't know why any woman would want an Indian workin' in her house, anyway, but there ye have it!" He laughed bawdily and cocked his thumb toward the prison. "Take some friendly advice," he leered, "if you find yourself inside, pretend you don't speak the language, and they might set you free, too!"

"We demand a hearing immediately," someone shouted.

"You'll get your bloody hearings soon enough," sneered the jailer.

"When? Where?" asked the elderly woman.

"This afternoon, at the meetinghouse," I said, surprised by the sound of my own voice raised among the protesters.

"Does your father know you're here?" taunted the jailer. "Don't imagine it goes well with Jonah Pryor standin' for election and all that his daughter consorts with a prisoner!"

"Leave the girl alone!" said one of the men.

"We want to see the marshal!" said the woman beside him.

"We want to see the prisoners!" shouted some of the others.

The jailer responded with a rude remark, and his audience responded in kind. Downhearted, I turned to go, knowing that I must tell Father the truth, beg his forgiveness, and pray that Will would be set free.

These thoughts were weighing heavily upon me when the squaw stopped me by the arm. Her baby, quieted now, was in her arms. Quickly, wordlessly, she began walking away. Clearly, she wanted me to follow. While the protesters and jailer continued taunting one another, that is precisely what I did. I followed her to a small lane at the back of the prison. A tall, spiked fence enclosed what I knew to be the prison yard—the place where prisoners were whipped, and worse.

"He is here," said the squaw in strange-sounding but distinctly English syllables.

"Will? Will Stoddard?"

"Yes. Will Stoddard," she replied, carefully repeating his name and pointing to a loose plank just wide enough for someone small to fit through, someone like me. She lifted the plank slowly, carefully, and looked to see if anyone was about. She nodded, so I hiked up my skirt, and squeezed through. At first, I could scarcely breathe for fear of being discovered.

"There," she said, pointing a long finger toward a tiny, iron-barred window just above ground. It was but a short distance away, so I ran to it and dropped to my knees. First, I listened for sound. All was silent. Then, I peered as hard as I could through blackness. Dank air rose from inside and touched my skin. I whispered Will's name. There was no response. My heart thumped as I looked around the empty yard. Deathly silent it was. My breath made flags of clouds in the cold morning air. I gripped the iron bars. "Will," I said again, louder.

I looked hard, just able to make out a figure rising from the floor. The figure moved forward—as far as the chains that bound ankles and wrists would allow. I drew in a quick breath. It was Will.

"Are you hurt?" I cried softly.

"How did you find me?" he said.

"When Father told me about your arrest, I came immediately, and this Indian woman, the one we saw in the wood, led me to you." I looked gratefully back at the squaw and turned again to Will.

"Are you all right? Have they hurt you?"

"I am unharmed, Hannah. It is rank in this cell, but they haven't put a hand to me yet. I think they mean more to scare than to injure."

"Father says there is to be a hearing today. I will go and tell the truth that this is all my fault."

"Say nothing, Hannah! I will explain that I happened upon the meeting by chance and will leave your name out of it. I have done nothing wrong, and they will let me go."

"Oh, Will! It is I who should be in your place!"

"I thank God you are not."

"I must go to Father. He will help—"

"He will never help me. And I fear he will send you away. Say nothing!"

"Oh, Will, what can I do?" I wailed.

"Go to Mary Dyer. These walls are thin. I overheard the guards last night. They know where the next meeting is to be held. They plan to lay in wait for her at the edge of the Duxbury village.

"How do they know her whereabouts? How did they know about you? Was it really Goody Hawkins who told?"

"Indeed it was. Goody Hawkins knows all about Mistress Dyer's movements. She made a bargain with the magistrates that she'd give them information if they'd let the squaw go. Some kind of trouble with Mistress Hull that could have put the squaw in the House of Correction for a very long spell."

"I don't understand. Why did Goody Hawkins not report me as well?"

"She's been waiting to turn the tables on me ever since she came beggin' in the tavern and I sent her on her way."

"The magistrates believed her?"

"When they came for me, I told them the truth, yet they dragged me off and threw me in here."

"Oh, Will," I moaned.

"It's no matter now, Hannah. I tell you, the feeling is fierce about Mistress Dyer. Believe me, *she's* the one they want. *She* is the one with the death warrant on her."

"How am I to warn her? What can I possibly do?"

"Tell the squaw. See if she can take you to Mary Dyer. She knows the wood and she is a 'Friend.'"

"I don't understand! Why do you to wish to help Mistress Dyer when you say she's—"

"Because this place isn't fit for a dog!" he cut in, "even a mad one! I have no blood lust in me like some others."

I put my head in my hands. Things were happening too quickly. Never before had I felt so torn between duty and conscience. Should I run straight away to Father and beg him to help Will—or to Mary Dyer and warn her!

Suddenly, I felt the light hand of the Indian squaw on my shoulder. "Go. Now!" she said. I sprang to my feet. We heard voices outside the enclosure and held still until they passed through the alley. From the tops of the pikes they carried I could see that they were guards.

"Go, Hannah, quickly," pleaded Will.

I said good-bye to him with great anguish knowing that my actions had brought him to this place. At least I knew that he was unharmed. In that I could take some relief. I followed the squaw back into the alley. When we gained the corner at Prison Lane, I looked at the jailer and the handful of people who remained at their vigil. Another guard had joined him. He was pointing at us and shouting something I could not hear.

Before I could think further, I found myself running through the winding lanes of Boston on the heels of an Indian squaw whose name I did not know and to a place I knew not where, for I had decided in that instant to do what Will had asked. I would go to Mary Dyer. If the squaw could help me, I would go to Mary Dyer and warn her of the danger to her life.

The town was not yet fully awake and the streets were thankfully empty. We ran on until we reached the Cornhill Road at a juncture outside of town square where we stopped a moment to rest, although my guide was not nearly as winded as I. As far as I could tell, no one had followed. Perhaps they thought us not worth the trouble;

perhaps they were glad to be rid of the sight of us. I turned to the squaw.

"Mary Dyer," I said. "Can you take me to Mary Dyer?"

She nodded in understanding. In that moment, a pact was made—a pact with an Indian to warn an outlaw. Should anyone know of this, should my friends see me in flight with this dark, ragged woman, I would have been greatly ashamed. Yet, I gave little thought to shame and regret when she touched my arm gently and said, "Come." Some divine Providence had brought me to this fate, and I surrendered myself to it.

The squaw took me to South Cove. Since it was well past daybreak by then, the cove was empty of fishermen who had already set out to sea for the day's work. This was good fortune, for surely I wished not to meet Joshua Grafton or any other of Father's acquaintances. The squaw moved swiftly, leading me to a small inlet where a birch bark canoe lay ashore. In one smooth motion, she pushed the small boat into the water and motioned to me to get in. I had never before been in an Indian canoe. The only vessel I had ever boarded was the Charlestown ferry, wide and flat compared to this teetering thing. I was terrified it would take in water. I heard tell that Indian children learn to swim at birth, but I certainly could not. Nevertheless, I decided that I must put my faith in God and in my new companion. I took small steps to the front of the canoe while she settled effortlessly into the rear.

With my hands fast on either side to steady myself, with my eyes fixed straight ahead, not daring so much as to turn my head this way or that, we were soon slicing the water to the rhythm of the squaw's strong, even strokes. The salty wind stung my face and dampened my hair and cap. There was no turning back; I would listen to the silence and face whatever was to come. I thought about Father and the anger and worry I was causing him now, but I had decided that, like my mother, I would not betray Mary Dyer in her hour of need.

It was some time before I began to relax my grip. I even summoned the courage to look over my shoulder at the squaw. It was the first time I had studied her in the full light of day. Her hair was long and neatly braided down her back. Her dress was of rough muslin cloth and she wore a coat of fur—otter fur I thought, having seen Indians trade all sorts of animal skins at market. It clung loosely, showing well-shaped arms. Her infant, bundled now on her back, stirred not a bit. Oddly, I felt comfortable in her presence. I sensed a boldness about her, which caused me to wonder what it was like to live among her strange people who moved from place to place, subject to the laws of the colony and the white man, yet above them at the same time. I looked along the shoreline imagining what everyday life must be like in an Indian village. I have heard tell that Indian men make their squaws plant and beat and barn their corn and build their wigwams for them. I had never dared contemplate their lot too much before, lest it cause me to entertain wanton thoughts. Now, I was more curious than ever. Who was she? Who was her husband? What had brought her to seek shelter in the home of Goody Hawkins and guidance in the church of Mary Dyer?

"What is your name?" I asked, not expecting to be understood but wishing to try.

"Mionie," came the swift reply.

"And I am Hannah."

"Yes...Hannah," she repeated solemnly, as if to say, "I know." I groped for something else to say but came up empty-headed. It was Mionie who broke the silence. Pointing toward the horizon, she called out, "Great, floating bird!"

I looked up, but all I could see through the mist were a few ordinary sea gulls. I looked harder toward the grey horizon, where the sea meets the sky in a barely perceptible line. I could just make out the form of a clipper ship.

"Why, yes, I see!" I said excitedly. "A great floating bird!" I looked back to show Mionie that I understood and together we laughed at the rightness of the image. It was the first time I had seen her smile and laugh, and it surprised me to think that we could share an amusement.

"The jailers," I said. "Did they mistreat you?"

She gave no answer.

"Do you understand why you were taken to Boston Prison?"

She looked at me blankly, then looked away, paddling with even greater effort than before, finally turning the bow toward a marshy rivulet. We traveled the rivulet for some time, reaching another cove where she steered the canoe onto a rocky bank. We got out. My shoes were sopping wet by now and water had crept halfway up my skirt. My companion looked not nearly as drowned as I did. I blew on my hands to warm them.

"Is she here?" I asked. Is the mistress here?"

Mionie pointed toward a path and stood motionless by the boat. I took this to mean that she was to wait for me there, whereupon I walked a short distance to a tiny village—an English village—that sat right on the edge of the sea. It held a most spectacular view of the vast and wild ocean, so unlike the usual calm of Boston's great bay. The place seemed deserted as though, like the Pequot village that Will had shown me, smallpox had claimed its inhabitants.

Keeping to the path through prickly hollyhock and boxwood, I reached a narrow stretch of sand. There, a solitary woman strolled over wave-worn pebbles blanketing the wet ground. The water lapped the shore in great weary sighs. The woman walked slowly. She appeared to be in deep contemplation.

"Mistress?" I said gently, wishing not to startle.

It was Mary Dyer who turned around, yet it was I who was startled, for she looked ever so much older and so terribly sad. Still, she smiled when she recognized me. It was like the sun breaking through dark clouds.

"Why, Hannah Pryor? What brings you here?"

"I have come to warn you, Mistress." I tried to sound reasonable, like an aged person and not a foolish, excitable girl. "You are in grave danger."

Certainly I had come to know Mistress Dyer as someone not easily given to fright, but I thought that my presence here in this strange place so far from home would cause her some alarm. I was mistaken. She only continued to stroll and smile as if to say, "Why do you fret so."

"Mistress, several people sit in Boston Prison as we speak," I said, trying to make her understand. One of them is my friend, Will Stoddard. He has sent me to warn you. The magistrates know that you are in the colony and guards have been ordered to lay in wait for you. They know when and where your next meeting will take place. You must return to Portsmouth Colony at once!"

"I am grateful to you for coming here, and I am deeply sorry for your friend, but the message you bring only strengthens my resolve. I cannot return to Portsmouth Colony."

I put my hand to her arm to stop her, and faced her squarely. "Surely you must go! There is a death warrant on you!"

"I understand the seriousness of the charges, child, but there is something *you* must understand. It is not mercy I seek, but justice. Innocent lives have been taken. Unjust cruelties continue. And still the laws do not change. My reprieve from the governor served only as a deceit to the entire world, and I must redress it. I can do no less than to warn our leaders to put away the evil of their doings before they lose all hope of salvation."

If dropping to my knees on the wet sand to plead with her would have helped, I would have done so. But the fierce blue of her eyes had returned and it made me dumb. I knew not what force of nature possessed her, only that I had never seen such valiancy in any person before, man nor woman.

"When my hour has come, I will proceed to Boston," she said with finality. "It is God's will."

I knew then that the hour was near. She will walk straight into the lion's den, I thought, and no one will have the power to stop her.

Chapter Thirteen

Consequences

The court hearings kept Father away until well into the night, and I had been long in my bed upon his return. I listened to the trudge of his boots as he moved slowly about, hoping that he would not demand to speak with me. I peeked out from under my bedclothes. Should I rise and face him now? Learn the outcome of Will's hearing and face the consequences? Fear is a powerful thing, and I clung to the darkness, unable to keep from shaking. I had braved icy waters and risked the elders' wrath when I ran with the Indian woman to warn Mary Dyer, yet that night I could not summon the courage to leave my bed. It was but a short time before all was quiet below. With Father having retired, I pulled the covers up over my head, said a silent prayer for Will and for Mary Dyer, and shut my eyes tight against the night.

When I descended the ladder in the morning, I readied myself for news about Will and for whatever punishment Father had deemed necessary.

"Will Stoddard has been released," he said sternly.

My relief was so great that I turned my back to him, so he would not see my emotion and busied myself cutting the bread, or tried to, for I could scarcely control the trembling in my hands.

"The jury saw fit to acquit him since he has not declared himself a 'seeker of light'."

"Oh, Father," I exclaimed, unable to hold back my joy.

"I thought you should know," was all he replied.

"And the others," I asked timidly. "Edward Wharton, John Chamberlain..."

"They have been fined and released."

Praising the Almighty for these outcomes, I knew in my heart it was time to put things right about being with Will in the wood that day. My voice wavered as I struggled to find the words.

"Father, I have something to tell you—"

"It is I who have something to say to you," he interrupted, his voice rising. "You willingly disobeyed me by leaving this house and setting out after that...jackanapes!"

"Father, Will is not—"

"Silence!" he shouted.

Father had never struck me before, but his words had all the force of a blow.

"A daughter of mine begging at the prison gates!"

"I am sorry, Father," I whispered.

"You disgrace me by your boldness. You jeopardize my position in this community. And with the election so close at hand! I will have no more of it."

I lowered my head.

"You will not seek out Will Stoddard. I forbid you to be in his company."

"Yes, Father," I said feeling the heat of my shame.

"What worries me most are your misguided sympathies. You will be under my watchful eye until this entire matter is resolved. We will be purged of Mary Dyer and her kind once and for all and you will see their menace for the evil it is. Do not doubt but that *justice* will be done."

"Yes, Father," I said.

"Look not so wronged! My displeasure with you is great, yet I impose no punishment but what is simply for the good of your soul."

Oh, Father, I thought, if only I could tell you that I, too, wish the matter resolved. That not seeing Will is greater punishment than you know. That I long to understand this notion called "justice!" What I heard myself say in a meek voice was "Yes, Father, I am sorry."

* * * * *

Mary Dyer was not apprehended in Duxbury that day, nor on the next day, nor the day after that. It happened some weeks later right here in Boston soon after the spring election. Father was elected deputy magistrate. I summoned my happiness for him as best I could; yet I dreaded the day that Mary Dyer would stand before him and the other members of the General Court. I dreaded the day he would play a part in condemning her to death. In the meantime, the court's business kept him frequently away while the breach between us continued to widen.

It was at market that I learned of Mary Dyer's arrest. While the story was told and retold in many different ways with many different people claiming firsthand knowledge, the truth of it, from what I could gather, went something like this: she entered Boston alone and repaired to the home of Isabel Scott and her husband. Isabel Scott was sister-in-law of Catherine Scott, Mistress Dyer's friend and fellow Quaker from Portsmouth Colony, who happened also to be the sister of Anne Hutchinson. There, she had lodged for several days without molestation or incident. With no appearance of departure and the court's leniency tried to the fullest, a signed warrant from the governor was finally served. It happened quietly and peacefully. The marshal and but a few guards had simply approached the Scott home. When they presented the warrant to Mistress Dyer, she complied without protest. She bade good-bye to her hosts, donned her cloak, and put herself in the charge of the governor's men.

"It was all so ordinary-like," said Patience Burrows. "She's playing her part to the end. Like it's all been planned. It ain't natural."

"If she had only stayed at home and cared for her children, none of this would have happened," said Nellie Colburn, wringing her long, thin hands.

"All and all, it *is* a tragic day," said Constance Brown. "I pity her family so."

A small group of friends and neighbors had gathered about our wagon mostly to hear Father's opinion on the matter. They thought that as deputy, he might be privy to Mistress Dyer's fate.

"What will happen to her now, Jonah?" asked Joshua Grafton. "Another long walk to the great elm?" Everyone laughed except for Father—and me.

"She'll be brought again before the General Court," he replied, "where she'll be given another chance to have her say."

"That's more than fair," huffed Goody Burrows. "It's only 'cause her husband's rich that she gets away with so much."

"You mean it's only 'cause her husband's a cuckold that she gets away with so much!" said Joshua. They all roared again as if the matter were merely for their entertainment.

"Call William Dyer what you will," offered Samuel Plummer, "but he is loyal to his wife. Is it true, Jonah, that he sent a letter from Portsmouth by Indian messenger asking Governor Endicott for a pardon?"

"It was read at court this morning," said Father, which immediately caused the lot of them to clamor for details.

"He threw himself on the mercy of the governor—husband to husband," explained Father. "He asked that himself and his children not be deprived of his 'dearly beloved.' Said he hadn't seen her in this half year. Cannot say how it is that her spirit moved her to such great zeal and to so great a hazard.'"

"He thinks her mad, too!" exclaimed Goody Colburn.

"He ended it by sayin', 'Pity me, I beg it with tears,'" added Father.

"Imagine, a man blubberin' with tears!" said Goody Burrows indignantly.

The group tsked-tsked and shook their heads. Whether this was done in sympathy for an upright husband or with derision for his weakness, I knew not. Looking at Father, though, I could not help but wonder what *he* thought about a man who defended his wife even when she stood accused of a crime.

"Do you think the letter will win her a pardon?" asked Sam.

"Let me just say that the governor appeared unmoved by the plea," replied Father.

"What do *you* think, Jonah?" asked Goody Brown. "What do you think will happen to Mistress Dyer?"

"The matter is entirely in *her* hands," he said. "Remember, the sentence has been passed. It is incumbent upon her to either renounce her ways or promise never to return to the colony. If she chooses neither path, the law sticks."

I winced at the words, for I knew the path she would take: she would never renounce. They were fooling themselves to think otherwise. I watched them—Patience Burrows, Nellie Colburn, Constance Brown, Samuel Plummer, Joshua Grafton, and the rest, mumbling their agreements with Father, taking comfort in the leniency of the court and the rightness of the law. But what comfort will there be for Master Dyer when his wife is condemned a second time? What comfort will there be for her children when her body hangs lifeless from a tree? Did no one think of that? How can they go on about their ways so easily—Joshua to his salt cod, Sam to his pewter wares, the goodwives to bustling about for sugar or pins or a piece of lacy ribbon? If only I could think and act and feel as they did. But I did not—I wanted Mary Dyer to live! I looked out over town market at the good people of Boston—people I had known all my life, people I trusted for doing good and right. Was there no one who believed as I did?

That is when I spotted Will's head above the crowd. He was walking in my direction. Oh, no, Will, not now, I thought desperately. I pretended to busy myself arranging the settles and chairs so that Will would go away and not bother me at my chores. As he approached, Father swung a cabinet down from the wagon with a deliberate thud, eyeing him all the while. The threatening manner did not escape Will's attention.

"Good day, Master Pryor," he said carefully.

When Father made no reply I could see that Will knew something was wrong by the way he cocked his head at me. Father saw it as well and intervened.

"I'll thank you not to be botherin' my daughter," he said.

"Sir, I don't understand...," he began when Father cut in angrily.

"There is only one thing for you to understand," he said pointing his finger in the direction of the tavern, "that you are not wanted here. Now, good-day."

Will turned to me for some word of explanation, but I dared not speak. I looked away, but not before seeing the hurt and confusion on his face. Not once, but twice, I had wronged Will and it left me sorely.

"Good-day," I heard him say, feeling his eyes upon at me as he departed.

Chapter Fourteen

The Verdict

Mary Dyer was summoned to appear before the General Court on the last day of May. She was to be questioned by the governor and the magistrates at a public hearing, whereupon a decision would be made as to whether her death sentence be carried out or a pardon decreed. Her day of reckoning had come. That is how Father explained the tidings to me. That, and how I was to accompany him on the appointed day, so that I might witness firsthand the fairness and wisdom of those who would pass judgment. As I sat across from him inside the meetinghouse waiting for these very proceedings to begin, I thought about that day at the spring not so many months ago when the children played and the sun was on my face and the leaves rustled gently in the breeze. Before I had ever heard tell of Mary Dyer.

This day was different. The morning began unseasonably warm, made more so by the bodies that packed the room to overflowing. Even with doors and windows thrown open, the air was thick with sweat and toil. Hectoring voices and cries of babies fairly caused my head to ache.

"Imagine, all of this fuss over the fate of one raving woman," said Merry, leaning into me. "Still, it is exciting, isn't it?" Her face was flushed and her eyes bright as she gaped around to observe who was present. Mistress Winslow tapped Merry's knee to make her stop fidgeting. I admit, I followed Merry's eyes. Goody Burrows, Goody Colburn, and Goody Brown sat directly behind us. Joshua and Sam were there and so were John and Martha Ballantine, and our neighbors the Tishmonds. Many more were from outlying towns—Dorchester and Dedham, Watertown and Malden, and as far away as Salem and Ipswich, I heard someone say. It seemed as though every county had turned out. Even Thomas and Dorothy Keane had taken time away from the tavern to come. At the back stood Black Joseph. I did not see Will.

A hush came over the room as Governor Endicott entered followed by his magistrates—first his assistants then his deputies; Father being among them. He looked not in my direction. The governor and his assistants mumbled words to one another and adjusted their black longcoats as they took their seats facing the people. The deputies in their more simple jackets and leather breeches sat to the side. I could scarcely look upon Father. Instead, I set my sights on Governor Endicott, who occupied the center seat, hoping to detect a sign of his disposition. Perhaps something about the brow or the eye would tell me that William Dyer's words had had their full effect and softened his opinion. It was but wishful thinking. John Endicott was to my mind a man of few sentiments, all of them severe. Watching him confer with Richard Bellingham and Simon Bradstreet only confirmed the gravity of the situation. Heads huddled close together, they made me think of Caiaphas and the high priests at the tribunal of Jesus. The faces of the other assistants revealed little more except that they looked ever so cross and irritable in their stiff white neckbands on this moist day. One or two of them mopped their brows with a handkerchief. Joseph Weld drummed his fingers nervously on the long board. Eventually,

I made myself look to Father. He sat with arms folded and eyes fixed not on the congregation but straight ahead, at a blank wall.

At the sound of commotion, I turned around to see Mistress Dyer appear in the doorway. She was being led in by two guards and followed by several more. Her wrists were bound by chains and her hair and cap were somewhat askew, but otherwise she was composed, just as I had expected. What struck me most was how small and inconsequential she looked in the midst of it all. When she reached the front of the meetinghouse, she turned and smiled at her companions in the front row, the Scotts, who had courageously housed her these last several days, took her place at the bar, and faced her accusers. Suddenly, all was as quiet as the graveyard. Infants slept as though not a word was meant to be missed; the goodwives ceased their whisperings; and even Merry for once lent a respectful ear.

The governor lowered his spectacles and looked Mistress Dyer up and down. He seemed as startled by her change in appearance as I had been when seeing her walk the sand in the village by the sea.

"Are you the same Mary Dyer that was here before?" he asked.

"I am the same Mary Dyer that was here at the last General Court," she replied.

"You will own yourself a Quaker, will you not?"

"I own myself to be reproachfully called so," she answered.

"She is a vagabond!" someone shouted, immediately setting off the congregation. Name-calling competed with demands for mercy until the governor intervened with his gavel.

"Silence!" he roared, bringing it down again and again. I feared that he would have the guards move against the whole lot of us if folks did not regain their reason quick enough. But as John Endicott was still a mighty commander, the pound of his gavel was all that he needed to restore order. When everyone had quieted, he continued.

"We have endeavored in various ways to keep you and your followers from amongst us. Neither whippings, nor imprisoning, nor banishment, however, would cease your purpose. What say you now for yourself before this court?"

Mistress Dyer raised her chin and said in a strong voice, "I came in obedience to the will of God to the last General Court desiring you to repeal your unrighteous laws of banishment on pain of death; this is my work now and my earnest request. Repeal them or others will come to witness against them even after I am gone."

"Are you a prophetess?" he sneered.

"I speak the words that the Lord speaks in me," she replied.

There was a profound hush from the crowd, lasting just long enough for the full meaning of her words to settle upon the witnesses' minds. Just long enough for the word "blasphemy" to form from the mouths of the goodwives behind me. The word passed from one person to the next. Louder and louder it rose, traveling the room like an evil spirit in flight.

Governor Endicott must have felt that spirit, for he rose, pounding his gavel again, his face turning the color of raw meat.

"Give ear and hearken now to what I say," he bellowed. "A sentence has been passed upon you by the General Court and now you will be returned to prison and there remain until nine o'clock tomorrow. From thence you will go to the gallows and there be hanged until you are dead."

The crowd erupted again, the governor hammered away, and Mary Dyer stood perfectly still. "This is no more than what was said before," she answered.

The governor leaned over the board to get as close to her as he could. "And now it is to be executed," he hissed.

All of the magistrates were standing now, including Father whose hands were clenched and eyes were searching the agitated crowd as the governor, gesturing wildly, ordered, "Away with her! Away with her!"

Several guards moved in, seizing Mistress Dyer roughly by the arms. The crowd was on its feet. The governor and magistrates swept hastily out of the meetinghouse by the side door. Through the confusion, I saw Mary Dyer look over her shoulder at the distraught faces of the Scotts as she was taken away.

What I felt at that moment, I cannot now say. I am uncertain that I felt anything at all, so quick came the decision. Nary a mention of William Dyer's plea nor the Dyer children, nary a word of debate from the magistrates about the rightness of the law. It was as though all had been decided beforehand just as the reprieve had been. What I do remember is feeling Mistress Winslow's hand upon my shoulder and her voice saying to Merry and me, "Come, come away now," and she was quite right for Mary Dyer was gone, tempers were high, and there was no use in our standing there hapless amid the confusion.

"Is that all there is to an inquisition, Mother?" asked Merry, showing her disappointment. "I thought it would last for hours!"

"Hush, child. It is finished," she answered, prodding her daughter to move along. "Be thankful that it is so."

Merry tried to ply her high spirits on me. "Hannah!" she said, wearing her mischievous smile, "you look as though you've seen the devil! Or a witch!"

I know not what kind of face I returned, but Merry looked exasperated and promptly left my side to catch up with the Pollard sisters and some other girls of our acquaintance to twitter about the judgment. I bade Mistress

Winslow and the goodwives good-day, for I wanted to be free of their watchful eyes to observe for myself the pandemonium that had spilled out of doors. A good many followed in the wake of the military guard taking Mistress Dyer back to Boston Prison. I feared that violence would break out, so forceful was the feeling in the air. I looked about for Father. I wished to find him and leave this place immediately, but he appeared to be in a heated discussion with several fellow deputies. I decided then to wait for him in the wagon. As I made my way through the crowd, I came upon a man holding forth a scroll.

"Your mark, please," said the stranger. "A petition to the governor to spare her life..."

I stopped to watch him as he turned this way and that, trying to gain the attention of anyone who would listen. Some folks signed their names; others brushed past him. Then, he held out the scroll to me.

"No, I cannot...," I stammered.

"Please, miss..."

"It does no good. I am only a girl..."

"The document has no legal binding. We wish only to make known to the governor the sentiments of many of us ordinary folk."

Before I could respond, John and Martha Ballantine had stepped in, hastily making their marks on the scroll without a word to either the man who offered the pen and ink, or to me. Eyes lowered, they moved off quickly as though not wishing to be seen performing such an act. I watched as others did the same. One by one, people I knew came forward to sign the petition—Joshua, Sam, and Thomas and Dorothy Keane. I was astonished to learn that there were others who wished her to live! There were people like me—Puritan men and women who wished her to live! This heartened me greatly. In that moment I knew what I must do. I stepped forward, took the quill, dipped it in the inkpot, and began to form the swirl of the letter "H," when I was stopped, suddenly, by the firm pressure of a hand around my upper arm.

"Come, daughter," I heard Father say in a flat, lifeless tone. These two words told me there was no need for explanation at present. I followed him, fairly running to keep pace with his powerful strides, stretched longer than usual by what I knew to be anger. Even those in his path seemed to know it, too, for they instinctively cleared the way. Challenger's reins were already tight in his hands by the time I had reached the wagon and scrambled onto the seat beside him.

"Have you taken leave of your senses?" he said. "Do you know what would have happened had you signed that petition?"

I opened my mouth to speak, but Father supplied his own answer. "My expulsion from the General Court or excommunication from the church! They will censure anyone associated with that petition! Do you understand?"

I knew not where I found the courage, but to my surprise I heard my voice say, "I must do what my heart and my head command me to do."

"You mimic her! You mimic that blasphemous woman and you mock *me*! Your heart and your head will command you to do one thing, and that is to obey!"

"I do wish to obey, Father, but this execution cannot possibly be God's will—"

"What do you know of God's will? Are you more wise than our elders? I brought you here today to witness the justice of our proceedings. Mistress Dyer has been given every opportunity to save her life, and she has refused. If our laws are not upheld, our colony will be finished. All that we have worked for will come to naught. We will perish in this wilderness if we do not conform!"

"But Father, so many good and upright people have today shown their displeasure with the law. Cannot the law sometimes be wrong?"

"Our laws are God's laws. We are knit together. We cannot allow troublemakers to tear us asunder."

With that, he clicked his tongue in Challenger's language. The horse obeyed.

"Father, help her," I said, putting my hand to his sleeve. "Go to the governor. Go to the magistrates. They respect you. Ask them to let her live."

Oddly, the storm in his eyes passed, replaced with a sadness that deepened the furrow between his eyes. "Lately, Hannah, you frighten me with your ways," he said, more quietly now. "I fear I have failed you. Without taking another wife, I have not provided a woman of the house to teach you properly. I fear I have failed you."

"No, Father, you have not failed me," I said with feeling, thinking about the letter—thinking that he might truly send me away.

He shook his head from side to side. "Mistress Dyer has sealed her own fate. My pleading for her life cannot save her. And neither can yours."

He snapped the reins against Challenger's back to move us quickly out of the square and into Prison Lane where a large group of people were already keeping vigil outside Mistress Dyer's cell.

He looked at them in contempt. "I have not worked long and hard all these years to gain a place in our community only to have it crumble once again for the likes of that woman in there."

I was downhearted to think that Father's momentary softening would not allow an ounce of pity for Mary Dyer, and bewildered by his words, "crumble once again." Had he revealed more than he intended? If only he would tell me about those early days, then perhaps I could help him feel differently. Perhaps then he would try to save her life while there was still time.

"It must be a terrible thing to know you are about to die," I said.

"What do you know of death, daughter, death and suffering." There was anguish in his voice, and I knew I had said enough.

I looked back at the protesters outside the prison as they grew smaller in the distance, sorely wishing I had signed the petition whatever the consequences might have been. At least I would have done something. The only thing left to me now was to hope and pray. Perhaps, the petition will work. Perhaps, another reprieve will be granted. Perhaps. I could feel my entire being willing these thoughts as the wagon creaked along at an urgent pace. One thing was for certain—nine o'clock would come terrible early after another restless night.

Chapter Fifteen

Day of Reckoning

The first day of June rose in beauty. The night's mournful rain had ceased, leaving a soft mist that vanished slowly, unveiling an astonishingly blue sky. The sun was yet low, but one could see it promised to be the most perfect of days. Behind me, young children laughed and played along the banks of the spring under the watchful eyes of their mothers. There was a certain freedom about the women today, too. Something about the sway of the hips and the flush on their faces—the way they threw their heads back and laughed—told me they were eased by summer's approach. I tucked up my skirts, squatted on a bed of rocks, and reached in. The water had lost its sting. Making swirling motions with my hands, I listened to the murmur of the spring's steady flow, trying to think of nothing, nothing at all when suddenly, I felt a splash of water on my face.

"Woolgathering again, Hannah?" asked Merry with a laugh.

"I'm surprised to find *you* here on washing day!" I exclaimed. With the Winslow household well staffed with servants, Merry was rarely to be found at the spring on washing day.

"I came to find you, Hannah."

"Well, lend a hand, then," I said rising. Merry followed me to the washing barrel where my linens lay soaking. We each grabbed a stick with both hands and began jerking it up and down, albeit Merry did so rather half-heartedly.

"Would you come with me to the Commons today?" she asked excitedly.

"To the Commons?" I repeated, thinking Merry should know better than to ask such a thing.

"Why, yes, for the, well...you know what for...everyone will be there."

"I will not be there."

"Oh, Hannah, it's what everyone is talking about. There's no telling what might happen, and I do not want to miss it."

"You'll go without me, then, for I will not attend."

"Well, if that's how you feel," she said defensively.

"It is how I feel," I replied. How could I begin to tell Merry how I feel, I thought. If she knew what I truly believed, would she still be my friend?

"I'll see you at meeting on Sunday, then," said Merry. "I will tell you all about it."

"Yes, no doubt you will," I said to Merry's back as she ran off. One part of me wanted to go with her, to laugh and talk and be free of my chores. But not to that destination. And despite the lovely day the Lord had sent, in my heart it was pitch and gloom. I pumped the washing barrel sticks as hard as I could, not stopping for the ache in my arms, when Anne Bradstreet and her grandchildren stole into my view. As I watched her approach, I thought how odd that Mistress Bradstreet, who occasionally read her poems to us at the spring—beautiful poems about her love for her home and family—could have a most tender heart when her husband, Simon, the magistrate, had one of stone!

"Yes, Mistress Bradstreet, it is a fine day," I called out in response to her greeting. I tried my best to sound gay, but my voice rang hollow in my ear. I busied myself with my task, hoping that she would not be offended by my disinclination to chat. I hauled the dripping linens from the barrel, squeezed out as much water as I could, and began spreading them out on the grass to dry in the sun. Over my shoulder I heard familiar voices. Patience Burrows, Nellie Colburn, and Constance Brown were approaching with bundles of washing in hand.

"Mark my words," Goody Burrows was saying, "this will be the end of it. Stop the greatest troublemaker, and you'll stop 'em all!"

"I am not as certain," replied Goody Colburn. "It might achieve the opposite, causing even more to take up her ways."

"Oh, that this day would be over, and all be well again," said Goody Brown anxiously.

"It'll be over all right," quipped Goody Burrows. "Just deserts, I say." She looked to her companions for agreement and they obliged.

"Heretic."

"Jezebel."

"Devil's harlot."

Upon seeing me they hushed. This time, I knew exactly of whom they were speaking.

"Why, Hannah, child, these things will never dry...here...let me," she said, taking a petticoat from my hands and wringing with a might only arms the size of Goody Burrows' could muster. "Like this, child, nice and tight."

"Yes, Goody Burrows, thank you."

"Hannah," said Goody Colburn, "you'll be joining us for candlemaking Tuesday next, will you not?"

"Yes, of course, Goody Colburn."

"And for spinning the day after Sabbath," said Goody Brown.

"Yes, I will. I have not forgotten."

"All right, then," announced Goody Burrows. "We'll let you get on with your work. You're a good girl, Hannah.

Stay clear of the Commons, today, do ye hear? I'm sure your father has given you sufficient warning, but don't think that I don't know what you're thinkin'."

"I will not be going to the Commons today, Goody Burrows," I said.

"Well," she added with a knowing wink, "I know you tend to get funny thoughts in your head."

Shielding my eyes from the sun, I watched as the goodwives moved further down the creek, thinking how nothing changes, how nothing ever will. I sat upon the ground and idly wound my fingers through the lush grass, gazing upstream at the looming forest when it suddenly occurred to me that the dream of the woman in the nightdress had not returned to me for several weeks now. I was pondering why this was so when r-r-rat-tat-a-tat, r-r-rat-tat-a-tat broke my reverie. It was the sound I had been waiting for—the sound of Mary Dyer's appointed hour.

I rose to my feet. All around the spring women paused to listen. Even the children grew quiet in their innocent play. Everyone stood still for a time as the drumbeat persisted and drew nearer. Slowly, however, one by one, as though in resignation, backs bent again to fetch water, lift children, scrub muslin—all except for mine. I walked toward the small rise. Passing Mistress Bradstreet I heard her say in a choked voice, "Might life not be spared? Oh, death is a great thing!"

When I reached the lane, the scene before my eyes was eerily familiar—the same scores of drummers, the same guards on horseback, the same insults, the same pleading. The same town crier announcing, "...Mary Dyer to be hanged until she is dead on Boston Common this day by order of His Excellency..." The same madness. One look was all I wanted, but I could not find her amidst the mob pressed together like a wall. I held steady to my spot, my eyes searching where the guards were thick;

where I knew her to be. Finally, I was able to glimpse the small figure—the side of her still white cap and her fine profile. But in an instant she was gone. I walked a few paces, but my legs began to feel terrible heavy, and I simply stopped. My head felt light; I could barely stand. I shut my eyes against the sun and the noise and sank to my knees on the ground. It had come to pass. May it be God's will, I prayed, as soft clods of earth from horses' hooves pelted me indifferently from the muddy road.

Chapter Sixteen

The Decision

"Old England is becoming new while New England is becoming old." I overheard these words one day at market, but only when holding Aunt's letter in my hand did they resonate with any real meaning. Even while the people of Boston were growing increasingly uneasy about the treatment of the Quakers, the leaders were growing increasingly intolerant, especially Governor Endicott who saw to mete out even more punishments against Quakers and their sympathizers. Mary Dyer had been dead these several weeks now, but others continued to come in her place, just as she had predicted.

"Better days await us," the letter had said. Of late I had been turning my thoughts to England, to books and libraries and music and plays. I had not realized how much I missed my lessons with Mistress Gibbons. And keeping Father's books was not a thing to learn from anymore. I had grown weary of townsfolk and their debts and their bartering, and their petty looking out after every last shilling. I knew all that I wanted to know about the people of Boston. It would be so different across the ocean, where towns have stood for centuries! There would be so much to see and discover. Each new ship to arrive from England brought news about the expectant return of King Charles II to the throne. There was great excitement, we had been told, and hope for a greater measure of tolerance from the new king. It was said that he was a young man. Perhaps, he would not be given to dourness and brutality, I thought. Perhaps, better days did, indeed, await the people there, while in New England, the climate only filled with more suspicion and fear. It seemed that Father was forever at meetings and hearings. What time we did spend together was marked by the discord between us. I stayed away from market as much as possible, going only when Father truly needed me or to get necessary supplies, because I could not bear the ugly talk about the persecutions. I continued to attend meeting on Sunday, of course, but kept to speaking only pleasantries with Merry and Hetty at the Sabbath House, as I decided it best not to share with them my encounter with Mary Dyer. Will had not appeared at church for several weeks. I chose not to attend other gatherings, such as the Ballantine child's christening and Eziekiel Smythe's ordination. It is not that I cared little for my friends and neighbors. It was that my spirits were low and my limbs so dreadfully wearied. Father seemed not to mind that I stayed much at home. In fact, I think he preferred it so, seeing me content at chores, Bible reading, and keeping his books. He knew not the state of my mind and heart and I wished it to remain that way.

It was because I was feeling so that I went to mother's trunk one late afternoon. I reached inside, ran my hands slowly over the silken ballgown, and fingered the silver handiwork of the lookinglass. Turning the glass over I studied my image. Do I resemble her? Was she beautiful, I thought. She must have been in all her finery! The reflection, however, showed not a pretty face, but a plain one, with strands of dark hair sticking out of a simple, sullied cap. I tucked them in and pinched my cheeks to raise some color. I may be plain, I thought, but I am no longer a child. I shut the trunk and went to the door to look out upon the approaching dusk. The air was warm on this summer's eve, and the sky was alive with the colors of the waning sun. In that moment I made a decision. I would confront Father upon his return. Yes, the decision was made.

Back inside I stirred up the pottage in the kettle over the fire, adding a little more barley for thickening, but not bothering with the marjoram or thyme for flavoring. Being without appetite I cared little for the taste of things, and plain fare was always good enough for Father, who appreciated whatever food I prepared for him. Soon the thud of Challenger's hooves sounded in the yard. A few moments later, Father appeared in the doorway, stopping so abruptly that he startled me. Although the light was poor I could see that he looked at me strangely, and I tried to read his expression for meaning. It lasted but an instant before he leaned his musket in the corner and removed his coat and hat and hung them on the pegs by the door, as was his custom. When he sat down at his place, I could see that his face was ashen.

"You frightened me, Hannah," he said with a meager laugh.

"Why, Father?" I asked.

"I thought for a moment that you were your mother. You look so like her, there by the fire. I thought I had seen her spirit." He shook his head and scoffed at himself for the idea. I served our bowls and sat down. We said a prayer of thanks and ate in silence. After a time, I began what I had to say.

"Father, about the letter delivered to you some time ago…from my aunt."

He stopped eating and looked directly at me.

"I read it upon its arrival. I should not have done so, but I did."

"I see," he said solemnly.

"Father, I wish to go. I wish to go to England."

A shadow of surprise crossed his brow but he said nothing.

"It will be for the best, Father. I am no longer a help to you, only a hindrance. You have prospered well with your election to the General Court, and I do not wish to jeopardize all you have worked for."

I paused and tried to look into his eyes, but his averted gaze was concentrated on the fire. I continued.

"You must know, Father, if there were a petition tomorrow to protest another execution, I would make my mark. I would do more than that if I could to prevent another innocent person from Mistress Dyer's fate."

"I see," he said.

"I do not wish to see you suffer again as you did with my mother. That is why I must go."

Still, he said nothing.

I took a deep breath. "I know of Mother's association with Mistress Dyer," I said. "I know that you disapproved of it." He turned to me.

"Who, who told you of such things?"

"Goody Hawkins."

"She is a mischief maker and a wretch."

"I know also of the monster birth that Mother saw that night."

For the first time in my life, I saw Father look truly frightened.

"Now can you not see that the Dyer woman is the mouthpiece of the Devil!"

"Mistress Dyer denies it. She told me herself."

"Mistress Dyer! How do you come by reckoning with Mistress Dyer?"

"I have spoken to her, Father."

"You have had words with Mary Dyer?" he said in astonishment.

"I was with Will when we came upon her in the wood. I asked her about my mother and she told me the story.

Only, she said it was not the Devil's child. She said that mother's death was not God's punishment. Oh, Father, if you would only believe these things to be true!" I cried.

"With all that you tell me, daughter, I do not know what to believe," he said.

"If I *am* following in my mother's footsteps, then so be it, but I could not bear to see you suffer again for my sake. That is why I must go."

Father pushed his chair back and let his hands fall limply in his lap. I waited for him to say something. Beg me to stay. Tell me to go. Anything to break the awful silence. It was some time before he spoke again.

"She looked directly upon me," he said.

"Who, Father?" I asked. "Who looked directly upon you?"

"When they accused her of being guilty of her own death by refusing to repent, she said, 'I came to keep the bloodguiltiness from you, desiring that you repeal the unjust laws made against the innocent servants of the Lord. *My* blood will be on *your* hands.'" He put his elbows to the arms of the chair and leaned forward.

"That is when she looked directly upon me, saying, 'But for those who do it in the simplicity of their hearts, I desire the Lord to forgive them.'"

"Oh, Father," I sighed.

"When they led her up the scaffold, she protested not and simply said, 'In obedience to the will of the Lord I came and will remain faithful even unto death.' Those were her last words."

Father leaned back in his chair and closed his eyes. For a moment I wondered whether he were trying to hear the workings of the Holy Spirit within.

"At least in England my mother is remembered well," I said quietly, knowing the discussion of my leaving had come to an end. I rose to clean the board and rinse the bowls. When I had finished, I took the Bible from the mantel and handed it to Father. He searched the pages and searched some more, finally settling on a passage. I peered over his shoulder to see that he had selected the Book of Jonah. Had he remembered that the story of his namesake, with all of its fantastical occurrences, was a childhood favorite of mine? I pulled my stool close to him as he began to read. His voice had such a gentleness that night that I could almost imagine I was a child again, feeling like I used to feel, safe and protected.

"Now the word of the Lord came to Jonah," he read, "saying, 'Arise and go to Ninevah, that great city and cry against it; for their wickedness has come up before me.' But Jonah chose to flee away from the presence of the Lord..."

As Father read the story, I began to think on its meaning in a new light. My childish mind had thought it a story of disobedience and punishment. Hearing it anew, I realized something for the first time. God punishes Jonah by sending him into the belly of the whale, not for refusing to preach to the Ninevites as commanded, but for *despising* the Ninevites because they sinned. Jonah wishes for the sinners' destruction because it is in keeping with the Israelites' law. But God's law is otherwise. God desires the Ninevites to repent of their sins and live, just as he desires Jonah to repent of his vengefulness and be delivered. The story is not about sin and punishment, I thought, but mercy and forgiveness. Jonah found that to be true to the Israelite's law was to be false to God's command. Until God showed him a better way. This revelation gave me much comfort, for I began to understand that truth and falsehood are not always easily known, one from the other.

When the story was finished, Father closed the holy book and laid it on his knees, returning his gaze to the fire's dying embers. I wondered what he was thinking and what meaning the story had had for him this night. I rose and stood behind his chair. Slowly, I reached to touch his shoulder. After a moment, he responded by placing a calloused, work-worn hand over mine. I whispered good night and went to bed.

Chapter Seventeen

The Whispering Rod

I managed to get my letter to the ship's captain just before the *Desire* set sail for England. It would be several weeks before I could expect a reply from Aunt on a returning ship. Have patience, I told myself. Storms and shipwrecks and mishaps at sea notwithstanding—and God willing—I would set foot on London's soil before the first frost hardened New England's.

I had composed the letter painstakingly, wishing not to convey a message that would cause Aunt to think less tenderly of me. I searched, therefore, for just the right words, and as my hand is not as beautiful as hers, I dearly hoped that Aunt would find in the sentiments and not the form the happiest presentation of myself until we would finally meet. I wrote that I desired the love, protection, and comfort of my mother's sister and her family. While it would be painful leaving Father, times were difficult here, and I longed to learn and to see more of the world. Yes, I will come to England if she would still have me.

It will be for the better, I said aloud to the wind. Yes, it will.

Shielding my eyes from the sun that generously warmed Town Dock, I watched the magnificent *Desire* slip its moor in the bay. To think that it would soon disappear from view to become a mere speck on the vast ocean! I wished her Godspeed and that her passengers—and the letter—would reach the opposite shore safely and in good time. Only a few folk had remained on the dock to watch her depart, still waving farewell to loved ones, even though they no longer could see their faces. I wondered if these were final farewells or simply temporary partings. At that moment, the allure of faraway lands had not nearly the tug it did when I watched the ships sail at Father's side. I thought how easy it is to be brave when thoughts of adventure are only passing fancies.

I stood awhile longer watching the crew pull mightily at the ropes to hoist the great sails. Already a prodigious wind swelled them. Like great heaving chests, they breathed power and life into the *Desire*, filling her with the courage to leave the great bay for the open sea. Only when she reached the outer bay, did I turn to go, deftly sidestepping a flock of gulls that competed angrily for the remains of a well picked over fish.

Despite the brisk air off the water, it was a lovely summer's day. The sun sparkled on the waves and the sky was a delicate blue. It felt good to be free of jacket and shawl and to linger in the warm sunshine. I shed my cap, stuffing it into my apron pocket, and let the wind blow through my hair. I felt like running and so I did. All the quicker to get to market, for I had another errand on that day. I hoped to find Will Stoddard.

Just a few brief words with him was all that I was after. It would not matter to Father now if I did so, I thought, since I soon would be gone. I simply wished to tell Will about my journey and to say good-bye.

As I made my way along the busy Middle Road, past horse-drawn carts, children playing, and boys driving cows to pasture, I came upon a familiar figure wearing a tattered cloak and hood even on this warm day. She carried a large walking stick. It was Goody Hawkins. My first inclination was to hurry past the old woman, though it be uncharitable. Goody Hawkins' betrayal of Will still stung, and I knew not what kind of reception to expect for myself in return. I was mulling this over in my mind when I heard, "You, there. Dearie...a word with you."

Planting herself in the middle of the road, Goody Hawkins beckoned me to approach. I bid her good day. A small satchel was tied around her stick. It smelled of stinking fish.

"Ye put a letter aboard that there ship, didn't ye," she asked. "Communicatin' with them Quakers in England?" She added her wicked laugh.

"Why, no, Goody Hawkins," I said indignantly. "I have no communication with the Quakers. Why, I did not see *you* at Town Dock!"

"...Goin' the way of Mary Dyer, are ye?" she continued without waiting for an answer. "They hanged her, you know. It was quite a sight."

"Yes, I know," I replied uncomfortably.

"They may stop one with the noose but there will always be another!" she replied gleefully.

Her lightheartedness was an abomination, and it angered me enough to confront her.

"Why did you name Will Stoddard to the elders?" I demanded to know. "Do you wish to see people accused? Do you wish to see people die?"

"He called me a witch...he laughed and jeered like all the others in their high-minded ways...that's why I named him."

I felt the shame of this and began to offer my regret of Will's unkindness, when she said, "I practice my powers on whomever I please, whenever I please." Then, she gripped me by the wrist with her bony, dirty-nailed fingers, and whispered, "You see, dearie, you I protected. You, I protected for other things."

"What is your meaning? What other things?" I said, trying to pull free.

"I told you when I described the day you were born—you were the smallest one I ever saw alive—and I knew then that you were meant to know the truth."

"Goody Hawkins," I pleaded, "what is this truth that you keep speaking of?"

"The truth that only womenfolk like us can know."

The grip loosened and I stepped back. Her words frightened me and I recoiled at the insinuation that I was common with the likes of her. I did not understand her meaning nor did I wish to unravel it. I held her gaze for several moments and then a strange thing happened. Fear left me. Suddenly, I realized that Goody Hawkins' power lay not in black magic but in something entirely different. Remaining steadfastly outside the law and outside the community, she was beholden to no one and would play one side against another as easily as not. Godless, she had accepted no Christian hand to help her back inside the fold, albeit perhaps none was ever offered. Looking into her dulled eyes, I knew not that she be a witch, but rather, a poor, lonely, scorned old woman. And for the first time I truly pitied her.

She seemed pleased with herself for imparting her secrets to me, and I summoned a smile. "Yes, I said, "I know the truth."

She patted my shoulder and ambled off in the direction of the Cornhill Road for the long walk home. As with the *Desire*, I watched Goody Hawkins drift toward the horizon, wondering what great gale lay in her course, knowing that in all likelihood I would never see her again. I could not help but think that despite her strangeness she had the wisdom of great years which had shown her much. *The truth that only womenfolk like us can know.* Whatever her special meaning, for Goody Hawkins never speaks plain, I could not help but feel a kinship with these words given all that I had learned these past months. And yet, I thought, how did she know that I put a letter aboard the *Desire*? I shook my head, resigned to the mystification of Jane Hawkins, and turned my thoughts to Will and what he would think of this encounter. I quickened my pace and headed into town square. It would be so good to talk with Will again!

Gaining the tavern, I decided to run around back hoping to find Will in the stable where not so many would be about, when I came upon Master Keane. He greeted me warmly and seemed to know just whom I was after. "He's tendin' the horses," he said with a wave.

I crossed the yard and entered the stable. It was cool and dark inside, a welcome relief from the day's high sun. I smoothed my hair back from my face and retied my cap, which I had nearly forgotten about. Adjusting to the dark, my eyes found Will in a far stall brushing a beautiful chestnut mare. By the likes of her, I judged that there was a very important guest at the inn, and though she may have delivered her master today and could be gone tomorrow, Will was talking softly to her as though she were his own. I approached and waited for Will to look up. In a second's time, he felt my presence.

"Hannah!" he cried, relieving me of any qualms that I had done the wrong thing in coming. It was plain he was glad to see me.

"Has your father business at the tavern?" he asked looking toward the door.

"No, Will," I said with a smile. "I come alone." I stroked the mare's nose and she responded with a grateful nudge to my cheek. We both laughed as Will brushed her lustrous coat.

"I've come with tidings, Will," I said, "and then I must be on my way."

He stopped brushing and put on a serious face. I smoothed the mare's flank, feeling embarrassed that what I was about to say might not be at all important to him.

He passed the grooming brush nervously back and forth across his hand. "What tidings?" he asked.

"I've come to tell you that I leave for England. I have accepted my aunt's offer to live with her." There was a long pause. I walked all the way around the mare, letting him take it in, for he seemed much affected by my words. Facing him directly, I said, "It is for the best, with all that has happened here." Still, he did not answer. "I so do count on you to be happy for me." I looked at him pleadingly.

"I am not certain I understand, Hannah. Does your father urge you to go on my account?"

"No, it is my decision, mine alone."

"You have made up your mind, then?"

"I have thought long and hard on it."

Will looked down, picking hair from the brush. "You will live in a fine house in England, will you not?"

"Yes," I said. "And be given the learning that my mother received there," I added.

"That is good. Perhaps it is best then away from this wilderness." He smiled sadly and asked when I sailed.

"I will wait for my aunt's reply that I am to come to her and sail thereafter."

"Aye," he said. There was an awkward pause.

"I must not keep you from your labor, Will. I intended to stay only a short while..."

"Hannah, wait. Wait here," he said hastily. "I'll be but a moment." Tossing the brush into the straw, he bounded out of the stable through the yard and into the tavern.

I leaned my head against the horse's flank and imagined what Aunt's estate would look like. Perhaps, it will have a chestnut mare, and she and I will ride for miles and miles at a time across great expanses and untold beauty! Then Will returned, and I came to attention. He was concealing something behind his back.

"Close your eyes," he said.

I was barely able to contain my curiosity. I had received but few gifts in my life, but each one, no matter how simple, caused as great a delight as the one before, for I have always been partial to surprises.

"All right then, open!" he said.

I opened my eyes. It was a whispering rod, a gleaming walnut whispering rod.

"For people who are courting so that they can speak freely between themselves in a crowded room," he said.

I took the whispering rod into my hands. "The workmanship is fine," I said. In truth it was well crafted, but I knew not what else to say. I took the gift as a show of affection and it made me feel awkward, for I was uncertain that my feelings matched his.

"I take that as a compliment coming from a joiner's daughter."

"It is handsomely carved," I offered again, hearing the feebleness of my words and wishing he would not look at me so. "You will be a joiner, yet, Will. Wait until Father sees it! He will be pleased with the work!"

"Perhaps," said Will. "Tell him, though, that I mean no disrespect. I simply wanted to give you something...now that you are going away."

"Thank you, Will."

"A clumsy thing to take aboard a crowded ship," he said with an embarrassed smile.

"Or a useful one with so many about!" I said, to make him laugh.

There was another long pause, then, impulsively, I put one end of the whispering rod to my lips and raised the other end to his ear. "I will not forget you, Will Stoddard," I whispered into its chamber.

"I will not forget *you*, Hannah," he said not in a whisper, but plain and clear for all the world to hear.

Chapter Eighteen

The Griffin

The summer weeks passed quickly as I waited for word from England. Good fortune it was that the days kept me busy, for I found work to be the best remedy for the jitters when I got to thinking too much about leaving. I took water to crops and mended anything of Father's that looked in need of repair since he was no good with a needle at all. I preserved fruits and berries and prepared stores that would last him well into winter. Still, I tossed and turned at night what with all that needed to be done in order to leave Father in good stead; the worry of it more burdensome than the labor. To be sure, Father would bring in a boarder to help with the autumn harvest. But a hired hand would not be sufficient. What he needed, I thought as I lay awake in my bed, was someone to manage his household; what he needed was a wife. It was high time. It was not seemly for a man to be too long without a helpmate, and goodness knows, there were many a widow and spinster in the town of Boston alone who would welcome the opportunity of a union with Jonah Pryor. In fact, there were eligible women, members of our own church, whose attributes I had begun to examine in great detail.

Waiting for meeting to begin on Sunday provided a good opportunity for observing. I started with the widows. Sarah Osborne was one. She had piety and a polite and tender nature. When we rose for Psalm singing, it was her voice my ear sought, for it was most spiritually arousing. And no one, not even Patience Burrows, made as light a pie crust. On the whole these attributes should have been enough, yet I had misgivings. She was of greater years than Father and from time to time was given to moroseness, as though some great sadness was never far from her mind. Perhaps, she grieved her husband still, though a more cussed man I have yet to meet. No, she was not suitable for Father. He would need someone of great and good cheer when I was gone. That she had three sons who doubtless would care for her in her later years made my exclusion of her an easier one to reckon with.

Beside Sarah Osborne sat Jane Farroway. Kind and as wholesome and sturdy as a pine, Widow Farroway had been left a sizable income by her husband, Richard, a master shipbuilder. I could not imagine her leaving her fine house, one of the largest in all of Boston, for our modest home, nor Father being comfortable in hers. I was glad then for her wealth, for it allowed me to feel less apprehensive when I considered that she had no chin to boast of and no talent with a stew or a sweet. No, Widow Farroway was not the rightful choice for Father, either.

Then there were the spinsters, Mistress Gibbons among them, whom I preferred to see better situated in life. At least the dame school mistress had an income of her own, though meager it be. While the others, Eliza Sorley and Prudence Hough, who without husbands, must depend on aging parents and overburdened brothers and sisters for their comfort and well-being. I wished I could believe that any of the spinsters would make a suitable match, but I could not, for one reason or another. A sinful admission, I know, but I did not reckon Father's affection for any one of them, even if it be said a hundredfold that husbands and wives come to love one another in time.

There was one woman, however, who to my way of thinking offered superior qualities. New to Boston Church, she and her mother had taken a pew directly in front of the Winslows, affording me an intimate view for study. She had well-shaped ears, a full head of hair, and appeared to be past the age of marrying young, but not too old to be deemed a spinster forever. During the nooning at the Sabbath House, I found her company to be most pleasant. She smiled easily, was eager to help with the serving, and seemed to have a keen mind. She was the only daughter of a wainwright and she happened also to be quite fair. I decided to broach the idea with Father one day in his work shed.

"Father, have you ever thought of marrying again?"

He raised a bushy eyebrow at me. "The thought, yes; the will, no," he said, shaving off a surface of wood with a drawknife. He continued working while I watched and contemplated how to proceed with this delicate topic.

"Do you not find Gissell Brenton to have an agreeable person?"

"I suppose she does, daughter," he replied. "Hand me the awl, the pointed instrument—there."

"She has beauty, wit, and industry, Father. Why not court her? You are not terribly aged..."

"Not terribly aged, daughter, but well on my way!" he said with a grunt as he pierced the wood with the awl.

"It is only right that you marry."

"I have little time for courting what with *other* matters to contend with," he added.

I abandoned the subject and left him there, working the drawknife more fiercely than when I had come in. I believed I had touched something sore, although I was uncertain as to which it was: Gissell Brenton or the "other matters," which I knew to mean the Quakers.

It was generally thought by everyone that the carrying out of Mary Dyer's sentence would be the end of it. No more Quaker preachers, no more followers. Even those who had shown a degree of remorse at her sentence thought it was all for the best. In the aftermath of the hanging, however, a very different story was unfolding. During those summer weeks, her name was whispered everywhere. "Mary Dyer. Mary Dyer." I heard it at market, at the spring, at meeting. At first I turned a deaf ear, but it was for naught. The memory of her, rather than diminishing, was only growing stronger. I even heard her name whispered among the trees.

All the while Quaker preaching continued and so did the persecutions. Whippings were reported to be regular occurrences—bloody, brutal whippings—women as well as men, Mary Trask and Margaret Smith among them, had been languishing at the House of Correction, kept from their children, ever since the day of the hanging.

Rumors, too, were flying as thick as mosquitoes in July. It was commonly known that Mary Dyer's family in England had strong connections to the king's court. Folks feared that if those connections prevailed, our charter would be revoked, and terrible things would happen—families would lose their land, prices would rise, the General Court would lose its power to keep us from unlawful behavior. In no time, the colony would fail and we would fall prey to the savages around us. This is what everyone was saying in one way or another, and it caused me fearsome worry. To my way of thinking, we were no better off with Mary Dyer dead.

There was, however, one bright prospect during these days. Word had spread that the governors of Plymouth and Connecticut colonies had written letters of protest to John Endicott, beseeching him to end the persecutions. I took this as a sign that reason would finally prevail, and I waited for it with great hopefulness. Yet, when I saw the governor about in town square or at meeting, he appeared to keep his warrior's countenance. Nor was the sign coming from the pulpit, for Pastor Wilson and Ministers Norton and North only continued to cry out against the Quaker menace. At the same time, a curious thing was happening. While there had always been a few voices to speak out against the hangings, now they were growing in number. I heard the evidence of it myself in many a public place.

At home, however, Father maintained his usual silence. He saw fit not to tell me of the court hearings that had sentenced more people to beatings and to prison. I preferred not knowing his part in determining their guilt and punishment, particularly when I discovered at the spring one day that another Quaker had been sentenced to hang.

His name was William Leddra, a devoted follower of Mary Dyer. Like Mistress Dyer, he had been arrested for preaching and given a sentence of banishment. Also like her, he had returned. Many believed there would surely be rebellion if another execution were to proceed. I could scarcely believe that it was happening again. Father said it would end. He said the problem would go away. But it had not. No one had been able to make it stop, and things were worse than ever.

These were my thoughts as I stepped down from Jonathan Tishmond's wagon. Jonathan had offered me a ride from the spring, bending my ear with rumors and opinions all along the way. I took him to be sympathetic to the Quaker cause, or at least against the killings, for he asked me not to tell Father he was distressed about William Leddra's fate. Still, he pressed me for information as though I might be privy to some confidential matter of the court. Folks were hungry as wolves for any detail on the matter. And Jonathan Tishmond liked nothing more than to be the bearer of news good or bad. That is why he surprised me when he said, handing down the water buckets from the bed of the wagon, "Why, Hannah, I nearly forgot with my carryin' on so about this and that. I've been to Town Dock. I've got a letter for you."

The letter! It had come! If only Jonathan could get his clumsy fingers to move quickly enough and free it from his shirt pocket!

"From the captain of the schooner arrived yesterday. The *Sparrow*, she's called."

I took the letter in hand. Even the many miles it had traveled could not damage its elegance—the fine parchment, the beautiful hand—Aunt's hand spelling out my name—Hannah Pryor. The first letter I had ever received! I waited for Jonathan, who seemed to linger, to finally cluck his tongue to his horse and pull away before I opened it, not even waiting until I got inside. This is what it said:

"London, August 1660. My dearest Hannah, having just received your letter, I write in immediate response. My heart is full of joy and happiness that you desire to come to us. I prayse God that He has seen fit to send you, and wish you a voyage free of peril in the hope that your departure will take place as expeditiously as possible. Please express my gratitude to your dear father with the assurance that our love for you will lighten any burden he might feel in your absence. We eagerly await you and pray for your safe delivery across the sea." It was signed "Your loving aunt, Lady Rebecca Waldron."

"And so it is settled," I said to Father later that afternoon. "I will depart with the next ship that sails for England."

Pacing back and forth Father had read the letter in silence. When he finished, he folded it carefully and handed it back to me. For a brief moment, I imagined that he would command me to stay.

"William Leddra has been sentenced to hang," he said instead.

"Is it certain, Father?"

"He will no sooner renounce his beliefs than did...the others."

"No doubt you are right, Father," I said with resignation.

"I fear there could be trouble in the aftermath."

"A rebellion, you mean."

"Aye."

"Then why not let him go!" I cried. "Why not change the law!"

"The law must stand. You know the elders' feelings on it."

"And, you, Father, what about your safety...how can I leave here knowing you might be in danger!"

"I am on the side of the Lord. I am not the one in danger," he said pointedly. "Do not concern yourself with this, daughter. Think of your own safety and that of your soul. That is what *I* am thinking of."

I tucked the letter into my apron and looked about the room, trying to focus on something that would keep me steady and from looking into Father's troubled eyes.

"I will take mother's trunk," I said, "and her belongings...if I may..."

"Oh, why, of course," he said wearing a look of helpless surprise, which pained me to see. "Do what you must."

I took a deep breath. "When does the next ship sail, Father?"

"The *Griffin* is in harbor at present. She leaves day after tomorrow," he replied.

"Day after tomorrow," I repeated, as though saying the words aloud would make the thing more real than it sounded to my ears. "On the *Griffin*." A monster, with the head of an eagle and the body of a lion.

"I've work to do in the shed," said Father. "I'll be back at supper." He took his leather vest from off the hook and swung it over his shoulder gracefully, just as I had seen him do a thousand times before.

"Yes, Father," I replied, wishing he would go quickly, because this time, I knew I would not be able to fend off the tears that were rising with a bitter sting.

Chapter Nineteen

Farewell

It is a wonder that I am able to recall the following days at all, for I found that saying farewell to people I had known all of my life put my mind and heart in a whirl. Exhilaration and fatigue took their turns on me. Mostly, folks had kind and encouraging words to say. But underneath, I heard sadness and a hint of fear. For it is the truth that the crossing is hard and once you make it, you are unlikely to return. For this reason I did as much comforting as was comforted. All of which can confuse a body unless one places trust in the Lord. Amazing what He sees fit to reveal to us when one door is about to close and another to open.

I set out for the spring early the next morning with yoke and buckets, two blouses, three petticoats, and one skirt that would be freshly laundered for the journey over. While the linens dried on the grass, I planned to walk to town square to see if I might find Merry and Hetty at home. It was a lovely late August morning with that clarity in the air that makes you mind the last fullness of the trees, the kind of day you want to hold on to, for you can feel the summer waning in the tiny shivering of still-green leaves. I must admit to lingering by the spring well after the washing was done, just to play with the children and listen to the gossipings of the goodwives. Patience Burrows was, as usual, full of news. It seems that James Thurgood had drunk too much ale at the Harrington's barnraising and had to be carried home by his wife and sister. Nathaniel Humfrey and Abigail Usher had been wed secretly. And for the third time in a month, Margaret Norwell's pigs had gotten loose and rooted Ezekiel Skinners' cornfield. He swore he'd start a suit against Goody Norwell if she refused to pay the damages this time, said Goody Burrows. Given how she enjoyed a bit of exaggeration, not to mention her talent for mimicking most folks in town, Goody Burrows had a way of storytelling that made the thing not a serious affair at all. So entertaining was she in the details that Nellie Colburn and Constance Brown laughed 'til tears streamed from their eyes. Not a mention was made of William Leddra. Perhaps they still thought of me as too young to hear of such matters.

Along with the gossipings, they made much of me—swapping reminiscences of my childhood. I felt a bit ashamed to have them go on about me so, but I thoroughly enjoyed the good humor. Being at the spring, talking and laughing together as we had done so many times before, taught me something very important. Though I would never be the midwife that Goody Burrows wanted me to be, nor work a needle with the skill of Goody Colburn, nor bake bread like Goody Brown, it was thanks to their ministerings that I had learned to manage a household. I had been the mistress and a worthy one at that. I thought back to the day that seemed so long ago now when they whispered words about Mary Dyer, which I did not understand. Now I did, and it made me feel less timid and meek—less afraid of the talk of women. I felt close to them and apart from them all at once, a hard thing to comprehend for sure, yet good and somehow right.

"You'll not forget us, now, will ye, Hannah," said Goody Burrows, pressing me to her ample bosom in a mighty squeeze that nearly took my breath away.

"Of course I won't forget you," I said warmly, setting my cap straight on my head again.

"I would have made a good midwife out of ye, girl, if you'd have stayed."

"Yes, I would have liked that Goody Burrows."

"I suppose you'll live like a duchess and attend balls and such...unlike us simple Puritan folk," added Goody Colburn, getting all teary-eyed.

"It is not for entertainments that I go. I hope to study and learn and—"

"But you'll remain an upright girl, won't ye, Hannah," interrupted Goody Burrows.

"Aye, of course I will," I said reassuringly.

"It's as though I was losin' one of my own," said Goody Brown, putting her hand to my cheek. I felt a terrible ache in my throat, remembering how she had made me a poppet when I was a very young child and sick with the fever— she, the mother of eight, had always found time for a motherless girl.

"Thank you," I said to each of them with an embrace. Saying good-bye to Patience, Nellie, and Constance was far more difficult than I had imagined.

"Go along, girl," said Good Burrows, huskily, "before we all get to weepin' so's we can't get our work done."

I knew that by the time I returned to pick up my washing, the three goodwives would be gone. All the quilting bees, all the soap- and candle-makings, all the spinning and preserving would continue in their capable hands season after season, without me. Their children would grow up and the three of them would grow aged together, God willing. And though I had faulted them uncharitably at times—Patience for her less than delicate ways, Nellie's habit of looking down her nose, and Constance's unceasing worry, as I turned to wave to them once more, I vowed to keep them forever in my mind's eye just as they were at that moment. Ruddy-faced, wide-hipped Patience; tall Nellie, willowy as seagrass; and the gentle, still-girlish Constance—linked arm in arm with their children all around them.

From the spring I walked on into town square to do the most difficult thing of all: say farewell to my friends. I stopped first at the home of the Shepherds at the back of Frog Lane. I had been to the Shepherd home on but few occasions, it being a humble place, home to eleven children with Hetty the eldest, and Mistress Shepherd not being one to hold a quilting bee or the like. She was a small woman with a pinched mouth and nervous hands. The Shepherds kept mostly to themselves. Master Shepherd had only recently moved his family from Topsfield where he had been a clergyman. For a reason unknown to me, he had lost his church and was looking for a new one. It was he who opened the door when I knocked. I could not help but notice that his collar was dirty and his eyes were bloodshot.

"Hannah Pryor," he said, waving me away with his hand. "Tell your father I'll make good on what I owe him. He needn't send you out after me. I'll make good soon enough—"

"Oh, no, Master Shepherd, I am not here on my father's account. I have come to call on Hetty."

"Oh, well, then," he said. "In that case…well…yes…come in then." He stood in the open doorway in a gesture I took to mean my visit would be brief.

Hetty was at table feeding the youngest in her lap. One of the little ones, Marjorie I think it was, stood crying in a corner, as did her older brother, who by the looks of things had been given a blow across the face.

Mistress Shepherd turned a look of severity upon me from her place over the hearth, where she was baking bread that had already begun to burn.

"Hannah," Hetty cried.

"Hetty," I said trying to sound pleasant and undismayed by the scene I had chanced upon. "I can see that you are occupied and I must not disturb you. I have come to say good-bye. I depart tomorrow."

Hetty looked at her mother pleadingly. While the severe look did not soften, Mistress Shepherd took the child from Hetty's lap and shifted him to her hip. She went on about her business at the hearth with nary a look or word to her daughter.

"In that case, Hetty, you can take this basket on out to the Willoughby place," said Master Shepherd sternly. The widow and her children are wantin' and they're dependin' on our charity. Go now. And don't be long. Your mother will be needin' ye back here."

I followed Hetty out the door and murmured a good-day to Master Shepherd as I passed. I could smell warm bread from under the linen cover of the basket. As soon as the door closed heavily behind us, his voice rose angrily, at whom I did not know, only that I heard his hand strike out at someone, and the children began to cry anew.

Hetty walked with me without saying a word. Though she tried her best to look unperturbed, I could see that behind that faraway look I had always read to be piety, was a hurt that she protected and refused to share, perhaps out of duty and maybe even a little pride. I squeezed her hand to let her know I understood and she returned first a look of surprise, then gratitude.

"I will go with you to Willoughbys," I said softly.

Hetty simply nodded her head and put her eyes to the ground. It was good fortune that at that moment Merry happened along. She was with her mother. It was a talent of the Winslows that they could brighten any day. I had seen it before. Merry and her mother had a way of putting just a touch of color in Hetty's cheeks and liveliness around her eyes. I hoped that they would do as much for her now.

"We'll all go, then, to Willoughbys," said Merry's mother. "No reason why we can't make a happy occasion out of a work of charity, now is there? Such a lovely day for a walk!"

Bless the hearts of those who, like Mistress Winslow, manage to find grace in impoverishment and bring lightness to a weary soul when needed most. Hetty's spirits lifted, we shared pleasant company all the way to the Willoughbys and back. Yet, when it was over, I was close to tears. To think that I might never look upon my dear friends again filled me with a sadness, which I had never known. That is when both Merry and Hetty promised to be present at the sailing of the *Griffin.* Having made a pact that we would be friends forever no matter what might separate us, and knowing that this parting was not the last, I was able to leave for home with greater cheer.

There was one other person whom I thought it only proper to bid farewell—Pastor Wilson. Since I had not found the heart to walk directly to his door and knock, Providence saw to it that I come face-to-face with him as I passed the meetinghouse on my way home. It being a Thursday, lecture had just let out, and he stood in the yard talking with some of the church members. I saw him watch me approach, but he gave no outward sign of greeting, causing me to think that he was perhaps uninformed of my impending journey.

"Good-day to you, Hannah," he said.

"Good-day, Pastor Wilson," I replied.

"I hear it is to England for you, my dear," he said dourly.

I might have known better than to think him ignorant, for Pastor Wilson is informed of most goings-on.

"Yes, Pastor Wilson, I sail tomorrow."

"Godspeed to you, then," he replied, patting me on the top of my head and extending a hand to the next church member who wanted his ear. I moved aside out of the menfolk's way, smarting perhaps just a little at pastor's abruptness. I watched him mop his brow with his handkerchief, a fine lace handkerchief embroidered with his initials, though it were hardly so warm as to display such discomfort. I wondered whether it was the same handkerchief he had used to hide Mary Dyer's face. I turned my eyes from it. May the good Lord forgive me, but this was one farewell that caused me little pain.

From the meetinghouse I walked on past the prison where a small group of protesters were keeping a silent vigil for William Leddra. Beside them, locked in the tight grip of a pillory, was a man, ragged and hollow-eyed, and barely able to keep up his head. A crude sign with the word "debaucher" hung about his neck. The sun was high and directly upon him and unlike Pastor Wilson, he was without a hint of shade. I thought he might die of thirst unless his time in the stocks were soon to come to an end. Little children ran by, taunting him and throwing stones. I turned against the sight and hurried away as quickly as I could.

Chapter Twenty

A New Beginning

The day of departure arrived heavy and grey. The air was thick with salt, and a low rumble of thunder sounded in the distance. Lightning spread at intervals across the sky, yet no rain came. I stood looking out the window, wondering whether the *Griffin* would sail in unmerciful weather, when Father entered from the lean-to dressed in his brimmed hat and cloak to guard against the wet that was sure to come. In the yard Challenger stood saddled and ready to take his master away.

"Don't fret, Hannah. If there is a gale on the sea today, the journey will be delayed," he said reassuringly, as though reading my thoughts.

"Yes, Father, I am not afraid, truly," I replied, trying to do the same for him, for he seemed agitated and in a tremendous hurry to go. I had found him to be strange last evening as well, especially when he told me that Will Stoddard was to take me to the *Griffin*. His own attendance was required at the execution of William Leddra on the very day I was to leave, but certainly I would understand, he had said. Ready to depart, he looked downhearted and perhaps even a bit blameworthy. "I will try to reach Town Dock in time," he said, "as long as my official duties do not prevent me."

Indeed, I tried hard to understand. Duty, no matter what its nature, is important. I had resigned myself to

Father's duty weeks ago. But if he could not take me to the *Griffin*, why Will Stoddard of all people! I wrung my hands thinking of our last meeting when Will's feelings were high. Truth was, I did not wish to face him again. The only sense I could make of Father's plan was that it was a peace offering to me over his hard feelings against Will. My spirit was as black as the sky. This was not at all how I wished it to be. I wished it to be a beautiful day. I wished Father to take me to the *Griffin* so that we would not have to say a final farewell here and now with my heart about to break!

Father held out his arms, and I ran to him. He wrapped his big cloak around me and we stood that way for several moments. Then, he let go. Before I knew it he had swept out of the kitchen and into the yard. I went to the window as he mounted Challenger, and with a sharp kick of his heels, they were off in a hard, pounding gallop. I stood pressing my face against the cool windowpane as I watched them disappear down the dusty road. I bit my lip hard to keep myself composed. I will see him again before we sail, I thought. I know I will.

I took my cape off the hook and draped it around my shoulders, for there was a chill in the air. I walked around and around the kitchen to see that everything was in its place. Earlier, I had fed the chickens and pigs and milked the goat, but returned to the yard just to look at them one more time. It was odd how simple, everyday chores suddenly seemed much more important. Will they miss me, I thought. Had these creatures been as comforted by routine as I? What will I do without all of this? What kind of person will I become in that strange, new place where people were living and breathing at this very moment?

The little mouse, whom I had not seen in days, poked its nose out of a chink in the wall as if not to miss its chance at good-bye. I smiled at the sight, grateful to the little pest, for I know I am given to thinking too much about myself, which can only lead a person to trouble. This was a flaw in my character that I vowed to attend to in my new life. The mouse slipped back into its hole. All was finished now. I was ready to go. I sat down upon mother's trunk to wait for Will's arrival. Closing my eyes, I asked for the Lord's blessing upon Father and this house and then listened to the silence.

At the sound of an approaching wagon, I stood and looked out. Will and his oxcart were pulling into the yard. At the sight of him, my spirits eased a bit. I knew that I would not have to fret over his state of mind as I would over Father's. And that Will would let me be if I felt not like talking. Yes, it was good that Will was taking me to the *Griffin*. I opened the door and stepped out.

"I hope the rain holds off for ye, Hannah," said Will, looking skyward. "Aye, I believe it will."

I smiled at his optimism.

"I hope you're dressed for the journey. Warmlike. Ye know the wind blows cold on the sea even in summer."

"Yes, Will. I have my cape," I said.

He came to the door. "Are ye ready, Hannah?"

"Yes, Will, I am."

Heaving the trunk onto his shoulder, Will went to the oxcart ahead of me. For the last time, I looked upon the only home I had ever known, straightened my shoulders, and walked out the door. I climbed onto the seat, folded my hands in my lap, trying, like Lott's wife from Scripture, not to look back. Only later did I realize that I had left the whispering rod behind.

We rode along saying very little. The swaying of the cart and the dark day lulled me, took my thoughts far beyond Town Dock and the *Griffin* to a faraway place, an unnamed place, a place where people were happy, where I was happy, where there was neither sickness nor cruelty nor death. I know it was but an idle daydream, yet I let my thoughts go to it for it soothed me. Every now and again Will cast a sidelong look to make certain I was well, and I would return the gesture with a fragile smile. He said more to me in those simple glances than if he had chattered all the way. I felt a kindness toward him that was as strong as anything I knew, and it made me glad.

My woolgathering was broken as we neared town square. Crowds were swarming in a line toward Boston Common. We took the opposite direction. I heard the drums beat and looked back to see if I could find Father atop Challenger. Was he thinking of me? Town Dock lay just beyond the square. Already I could see the tops of the *Griffin*'s tall masts. My heart quickened. Everything was moving with such great haste. Peace and silence were gone now that William Leddra's death walk had begun. I tried to harden my heart to it. Death was his fate and there was nothing I could do but say a prayer that it be quick and he not suffer. I had my own journey to think about at present and I looked to the road ahead of me.

Will steered the oxcart onto the landing at Town Dock. The drumbeat, fading in the distance, gave way to noisy sailors and squawking gulls. The dock's long, rickety arm reached well into the bay. Beyond, anchored in deeper waters, lay the *Griffin*. Choppy seas rocked her to and fro. I thought that a sailing ship never looked so fragile as she did on this day. I got down from the oxcart. Will was already at the back, hauling out the trunk. I handed him the four pounds for my passage, hard-earned coin from Father's trade, and watched him take the trunk to the skiff. Just then, I spotted Merry and Hetty.

Out of breath, running along the dock, the girls made a brazen sight, quite apart from their usual propriety, especially Hetty's, which only warmed them more to my heart. When they reached me, I took each of their hands while they said how they would not have missed the chance to see me off no matter how inclement the weather.

"Oh, how I envy your adventure, Hannah!" gushed Merry.

"How wonderful it will be for you to see England!" cried Hetty.

"Would that you were coming with me," I said.

Soon Will returned.

"All is in place, Hannah. Your trunk is with the stevedore, your passage is paid, and your name is noted on the passenger list."

"How exciting!" said Merry, clapping her hands.

I thanked Will warmly. There was nothing more to do but wait. Thunder sounded and a bolt of lightning creased the sky. A gust of wind blew dust in circles around us.

"Where is your Father?" asked Hetty with concern.

"With court business today," I replied, feeling the full weight of Father's absence.

"Oh, that...," said Merry with unspoken meaning.

"But he promised to try and arrive in time," I said, assuring myself as much as Merry.

Merry shrugged and Hetty looked at me with pity. "I know he will be here," I said. "I know he will."

Soon Town Dock began to fill with passengers and those come to see them off—all kinds of folk—farmers, yeomen, and traders with goods to exchange in England. I looked about to see if there were any acquaintances to provide companionship during the long journey over, but I knew none. Mostly they were men, undoubtedly with business to conduct in England. There were more than a few families, it seemed, two or three with babies and young children clutching their mothers' hands. I thought perhaps I could be a comfort to them and their young ones, knowing that I would likely be in need of their friendship before too many days had passed at sea.

Mostly, we watched the sailors load the skiffs. They stood in a long line, rough-faced men, passing cargo hand to hand—animal skins, lumber, pickled fish, and oysters by the barrelfull—and spices, tobacco, and sugar that had come north from the islands of the West Indies. Precious goods from the New World to the Old. To think that these are considered foreign and exotic in England made me feel at once both proud and sad. Through different eyes I began to see that I was a daughter of the wilderness. I was born of the same place that produced these gifts and I cautioned myself to never forget where my true home lay.

Soon signs of imminent departure were at hand. The crew had rowed the last of the cargo to the *Griffin* and were returning for the passengers. They rowed with great effort over waves that had grown heavier and angrier. Even the passengers' expressions seemed to strain now that embraces and final words had been spent, now that they faced the prospects of days and nights upon a roiling sea. Sailors placed a gangway from the dock to an awaiting skiff. People began lining up. A man whom I judged to be the captain by the emblems on his coat stood at the top of the gangway making marks in a book. An infant let out an alarming cry, and a flock of gulls mocked it with a baleful noise of their own. Already a dozen sailors had climbed great heights to rig the masts. I looked anxiously about for Father while someone shouted, "All aboard! All aboard!"

"Hannah, it is time," said Will, gently.

I bit my lip hard. "He must be coming down the lane by now," I said, standing on tiptoe and straining to see.

"Perhaps your Father finds it best to stay away. Perhaps it is too difficult," said the sensible Hetty, embracing me. "Godspeed, my dear friend, until we meet again."

"Yes, Hetty. I will write to you," I said embracing her in turn.

"Tell us everything about London, your entertainments, and of course, the many young beaux you're sure to have!" said Merry, squeezing me tightly around the neck.

"Hush, Merry!" I said with embarrassment, but smiling and brushing away her tears. "I have never seen you weep before this day. Be happy for me!"

"I am happy for you, Hannah. Would that it were *I* going to England!"

"Dear Merry! Vainglorious to the end!" And we laughed together for we both knew it to be the truth. Then I turned to Will.

"He said he would be here."

"Hannah, time is short. The captain gives the last call aboard."

Will was right. Father had only said he would try. It was time to go. Putting both hands on his arms, I lightly brushed his cheek with my lips and pushed quickly away. Gathering my skirts, I ran to the gangway behind the last of the passengers to board the skiff that would take us to the *Griffin*. I looked back at my friends. They were waving and shouting words I could not hear over the orders of the captain to the crew. The wind was coming strong off the water now. Stormy clouds hovered darkly and a thunderclap pierced the air. My eyes sought Father one last time. The pit of my belly turned like the ocean beneath my feet. My head swam with the waves. I thought I would swoon when above the din I heard the calling of my name, "Hannah, Hannah!" It was the sound of his voice. Father's voice. I knew you would come, I said to myself. I knew in my heart you would come. Gripping the rope on the gangway, I tried to steady myself when I beheld Father dismounting Challenger in one swift motion. The horse's nostrils were wide and its mouth in a lather. Father tossed Challenger's reins to Will, and I broke from my fellow passengers to run to him.

"Oh, Father!" I cried. He embraced me heavily with nary a word. I could feel trembling through the cloth of his jacket.

"Father, what is wrong!" I said, looking into his stricken face.

He lowered his eyes to the ground. He had difficulty speaking. "Daughter, I fear we have been murdering the Lord's people," he said, his voice choked with grief.

"Oh, Father," I said leaning my head against his chest.

"I can no longer have a hand in the slaughtering of the innocents."

I raised my head to him. "Father, I do not understand."

"I have resigned my position in protest."

"But Father, what will this mean for you…your church membership…your livelihood?"

He took my hands in his and in a stronger voice said to me, "At the death of William Leddra this morning, the Lord sent me a revelation, which is this: I must do what my head…and my heart…command me to do."

"Oh, Father," I said with such a mixture of happiness for his wondrous change of heart and utter dismay at its suddenness that I knew not what to think or what more to say. All that mattered now was that the *Griffin* beckoned and I had to go. I looked back at the gangway where the captain was shouting something in an angry voice and the last skiff waited with all the passengers' curious eyes upon myself and Father.

"Wait, daughter, there is something else that I must say."

"What Father, speak!" I cried.

"I desire you to stay."

I am certain I looked at him blankly, for it took several moments for his meaning to reach my ears.

"Your strength of conviction will be my guide just as your mother's used to be…before I refused the wisdom of her truth. I desire you to stay…but only if you desire it also."

The words were spoken. I was reprieved. I had been forgiven. At that moment, the stormclouds that had stalked and threatened all morning long burst overhead and water came pouring down upon us like a baptism.

"Yes, Father, yes," I said. Cold rain pelted my face as I looked into his deep, grey eyes. "I do desire to stay! It is what I have always desired!"

And then I laughed aloud in pure unexpected joy, and so did he.

Chapter Twenty-One

Forgiveness

Home together by the light of the hearth, I showed Father the whispering rod that Will had given me.

"Well done, it is," he said, examining the handiwork. "Will has the makings of a craftsman. Perhaps with a proper apprenticeship he will become one."

"Will's debt to the Keanes is nearly discharged," I offered. "With business growing the way it is, you could use some help and Will could be your..."

Father smiled mindfully. "Yes, daughter, your point is well made. I *could* use another pair of skilled hands. I'll think on it. The good Lord willing, he shall have his chance," he said, adding with a wink, "young Stoddard willing, too, of course."

As I stirred the embers in the hearth, I could hardly keep from smiling. How happy Will will be, I thought, when suddenly I remembered Aunt. Here I was filled with joy for my good fortune without giving a thought to the disappointment I was causing another—my own kin and one who had proffered her home, her protection, her love. I threw a few small sticks on the fire to keep the light from going out and stared into the dancing flames. Indeed, I felt remorse on her account for my change of heart. And yet I felt a contentment I had not felt for a very long time. Perhaps, I would journey to England one day, I thought.

Yes, I would like that very much; I simply knew in my heart that I was not ready to call another place my home.

"Did I ever tell you the story about the whispering rod?" asked Father.

"Why, no," I said with surprise.

"It is how I began the courtship of your mother."

Father courting Mother with a whispering rod, I thought! Father patted my stool, and eagerly, I sat down. Thus he began the story that I had been waiting so very long to hear. He started at the beginning—the day they met on the streets of London.

Each had stopped to listen to a Puritan preacher, Mother more out of curiosity than piety, Father added, smiling. He was immediately taken by her fairness, gaiety and wit, yet knew himself to be without prospects, she being a lady, judging by her elegant dress, and he but a lowly carpenter. Although she was not a follower, she wanted to learn more about his Puritan beliefs. He laughed to think that she was not at all put off by his serious ways, but rather was keenly interested in his devoutness, eventually matching it with a fervor of her own. They began courting, helped on more than one crowded occasion by the presence of a whispering rod. In time, they planned to wed, but because he was poor, her family did not approve. For this she was ready to forsake all—her material comforts, her family, her home. And so, with silver from a sympathetic uncle, she made it possible for him to purchase shares in the Massachusetts Bay Colony. They knew that making a home in the New World would be difficult and dangerous, but they were ardent in their faith and full of hope for a new society. Under John Winthrop's leadership, the colony was showing signs of great promise and fulfillment of God's will. Indeed life was hard, he said, with their numbers so few. Winters were severe and food often in great shortage. They toiled from dawn 'til night, day after day and year after year, contending with mosquitoes and pests, smallpox and fever, bears and coyotes, who in the blink of an eye would eat your crops and kill your livestock, or your child. They survived even these and worse—the terrible war with the Pequots. Yet despite the hardships, people kept coming and the colony grew. The more it grew, the harder it was to keep intact the original covenant—to build a New Jerusalem for our salvation. How difficult it was, he said, and how much more so when she quit the world, forever.

The tale lasted well into the night and in the telling something wonderful happened—a revelation which was as new to Father as it was to me when at last he said it— that the anguish he had felt ever since Mother's passing was not the anguish of God's judgment against her, but the pain of his having betrayed her memory.

"A godly woman she was, Hannah. Like Jonah, I was blind to the Lord's test. I just couldn't see what He wanted of me."

The story was finished. It was time for bed. I kissed Father's cheek and climbed the ladder to the loft, turning as I gained the top step to look down upon him as he thumbed the pages of the Bible in his chair by the fire. When he stopped at a passage, I knew by the parting of the book which one it to be—Proverbs 31, the story of Bathsheba. I changed into my nightclothes and slipped beneath the quilts, but did not close my eyes straight away. Instead, I gazed out the window at a sliver of the night sky, so perfectly clear now with stars glowing brilliant and white. Finally warm and content, I nestled down and said a silent prayer of thanks, knowing that for the first time in many years Father would "praise his wife." From now on he would call her "blessed."

Afterword

The last Quaker to be executed in Boston was William Leddra in 1661. Another Quaker, Wenlock Christison, was scheduled to be put to death the following June, but appealed his case to the English royal government. Eventually, he was released from prison and expelled from the Massachusetts Bay Colony along with twenty-seven other Quaker prisoners. Facing growing indignation from citizens of the colony and growing fear of intervention from England, the General Court repealed the anti-Quaker laws' death penalty in that same year. In its place, however, was enacted a new law called The Cart and Whip Act. This law provided that any banished Quaker who returned would be stripped to the waist, tied to the end of a cart, and whipped from town to town until he or she was out of the jurisdiction. Many of the Quakers released with Wenlock Christison were punished by this law. In the following year, 1662, three women were whipped the lengths of eleven towns through deep snow in December. Witnesses testified to blood freezing on their clothes as it ran down their backs.

Whippings and imprisonment of Quakers continued until the death of John Endicott in 1665. In May of that year, representatives of the royal government commanded that the General Court stop the persecutions. Although one could still be fined for attending a Quaker meeting,

Friends for the first time since their arrival on New England's shores could go about their business in relative peace.

In 1681, Massachusetts Bay Colony lost its royal charter to rule, and a new governor was appointed by the Crown. With England assuming direct governance, the Anglican Church became firmly established in Boston, essentially bringing Puritanism to an end.

The Puritan era lasted only approximately fifty years. While Anglicanism in Virginia, Catholicism in Maryland, and Quakerism in Pennsylvania endured as predominant religious movements for longer periods of time and with greater numbers of participants, we continue to associate ourselves as a nation with our "Puritan forefathers." Why has the Puritan legacy endured? Perhaps, it is for the simple reason that in this brief, powerful period, we find the very origins of what it means to be an American.

Today, on the lawn of the Massachusetts State House sits a statue of Mary Dyer. It is inscribed with words taken from her second and last letter to the General Court written while in prison awaiting execution. The inscription reads: "My life not availeth me in comparison to the liberty of the truth."

The statue overlooks Boston Common.

Bibliography

Bacon, Margaret. *The Quiet Rebels*. New York: Basic Books, Inc., 1969.

Battis, Emery. *Saints and Sectaries*. Chapel Hill: University of North Carolina Press, 1962.

Bercovitch, Sacvan. *Puritan Origins of the American Self*. New Haven: Yale University Press, 1986.

Best, Mary Agnes. *Rebel Saints*. New York: Harcourt, Brace & Company, 1925.

Bolton, Reginald Pelham. *A Woman Misunderstood: Anne, Wife of William Hutchinson*. New York, 1931.

Chu, Jonathan. *Neighbors, Friends or Madmen*. Westford, Connecticut: Greenwood Press, 1985.

Crawford, Mary Caroline. *Social Life in Old New England*. Boston: Little, Brown and Company, 1914.

Daniels, Bruce Colin. *Puritans at Play*. New York: St. Martin's Press, 1995.

Earle, Alice Morse. *Customs and Fashions in Old New England*. New York: Charles Scribner's Sons, 1893.

Hallowell, Richard P. *The Quaker Invasion of Massachusetts*. Boston: Houghton Mifflin and Company, 1887.

Hodges, George. *The Hanging of Mary Dyer*. New York: Moffet Yard & Company, 1907.

Holliday, Carl. *Woman's Life in Colonial Days.* Corner House Publishing, 1968.

Ilgenfritz, Elizabeth. *American Women of Achievement: Anne Hutchinson, Religious Leader.* New York: Chelsea House Publishers, 1991.

Miller, Perry, and Thomas H. Johnson. *The Puritans, Vol. I & II.* Rev. ed. New York: Harper & Row, 1963.

Morrison, Samuel Eliot. *Builders of the Bay Colony.* Boston: Northeastern University Press, 1930.

Nash, Gary B. *Red, White & Black, the Peoples of Early America.* Englewood Cliffs, New Jersey: Prentice Hall, 1974.

Nichols, Joan Kane. *A Matter of Conscience.* Austin: Raintree, Steck-Vaughn, 1993.

Paine, P. T., ed. *A Call from Death to Life.* Friends in London, 1660. Reprinted by Knowles, Anthony & Company, Providence, 1865.

Plimpton, Ruth Talbot. *Mary Dyer: Biography of a Rebel Quaker.* Boston: Branden Publishing Company, 1994.

Rogers, Horatio. *Mary Dyer of Rhode Island, The Quaker Martyr that was Hanged on Boston Common.* Providence: Preston and Rounds, 1896.

Rutman, Darrett B. *Winthrop's Boston: Portrait of a Puritan Town 1630–1649.* Chapel Hill: University of North Carolina Press, 1965.

Selleck, George. *Quakers in Boston.* Cambridge, Massachusetts: Friends Meeting at Cambridge, 1976.

Travers, Milton A. *One of the Keys.* Dartmouth, Massachusetts: Bicentennial Commission, 1975.

Tunis, Edwin. *Colonial Living.* New York: Thomas Y. Crowell Company, 1957.

Vaughn, Alden T. *New England Frontier, Puritans and Indians.* Boston: Little, Brown and Company, 1965.

Weeden, William Babcock. *Economic and Social History of New England.* Boston: Houghton Mifflin and Company, 1890.

Winthrop, John. *History of New England from 1630–1649.* Boston: Little, Brown and Company, 1853.

Yolen, Jane. *Friend: Life of George Fox and the Quakers.* New York: Seabury Press, 1972.